Creative Writing Short Stories

A Collection of Short Stories Written by Members of the Atria Willow Glen Creative Writing Group

Story Locations

Section One
Introduction to Ryker

Several stories written by creative writers in this book were about the character of Ryker Fleming, a Private Investigator. The stories below were some of the best.

Private Eye
By Chuck Northup

"The Defense calls Ryker Fleming as an expert witness," said the defense counsel.

A man well over six feet tall with strong features strode toward the witness box. He appeared to be in his fifties, with dark hair, and clear brown eyes. He was muscular with the calloused hands of a wrestler. He was a good person to have on your side in a fight.

In the witness box, he sat with assurance, while looking directly at the jury as he answered their questions.

"For the jury, please state your full name," instructed the counselor.

"Ryker Fleming," the witness responded, "but I usually go by just my first name, which is Ryker."

"Please spell your first name for the court reporter," added the lawyer.

"**R, y, k, e, r,**" he answered.

"All right, now state your qualifications for being an expert witness."

"After graduating from college, I was a member of the FBI for over ten years, and then for 12 years I was a member of the New York City Police Department, Homicide Division. I have also been in practice as a licensed private detective for the past five years. I have solved at least 25 murders, but who's counting?"

A titter of laughter came from the gallery, so the judge had to hammer his gavel twice.

The murder suspect, Gloria Divelli, was the wife of a real estate man who had died recently under suspicious conditions. Initially he had hired Ryker to defend her. As the old saying goes, the spouse is always the first one to be suspected.

Gloria had been married to a man with a reputation for shady dealings. Nevertheless, he had helped create the Feminine Protective

League (FPL), a charity that collected money to give to women in financial need, often due to walk-away or probation husbands, or under other similar circumstances. There was no nonsense required about written checks or electronic cards, for the women were always given cash, whenever they required it.

Mr. Divelli's body had been found in his own office, which had been thoroughly ransacked. The assailants, however, had not searched the inner compartments of the copier machine, where the authorities soon found several bags containing over $50,000 each in cash.

Ryker found that two other men, Bloomberg and Dustman, had the authority along with Deville to withdraw funds from the FPL. All three had been pouring money into it, although the FPL paid out very little to needy women. It seemed that FPL might have been a front organization for the laundering of illegal money.

Bloomberg and Dustman operated a firm called Richmont, which purported to be an investment firm. Investors expected to receive dividends of at least 18% and plenty of gullible people invested in Richmont, only to see their stock eventually fail and their money disappear.

Ryker thought that either Bloomberg or Dustman was more likely to be the murderer, rather than their client. Divelli had also been working his own scheme, using real estate values instead of stock values. The three men gathered one evening at the Rancher's Steak House to discuss business.

"This Bordeaux is a great wine with steak," said Bloomberg.

"It's okay," replied Dustman, "but I'd prefer one with a fuller body."

"You guys can worry about wine," declared Divelli, "but I'd like to know how much money you talk out of investors before their cash runs out."

"On a million-dollar property, customers will put up approximately $100,000 on it. I can then find 25 or 30 grand to hide in fees, and I usually then gain a client as a customer. He keeps coming back."

The Richmont men were envious of the amount of money Divelli was making, and when they conferred with him later that evening, they decided to take direct action to get some of it.

At first they thought it must be mostly in his office. They visited him there and demanded his money. He told them he did not keep it in his stock file.

"I suspect that most of our investors are new to this, and they don't want to put much money up to start with. They usually come up with only five or ten thousand," said Bloomberg.

"Then you have to start looking for another investor," suggested Divelli.

"Yeah," said Dustman, "but there aren't lots of them out there. What about you?"

"People normally put up larger amounts in real estate, and I can siphon off part of it," said Divelli.

"What do you call large?" asked Bloomberg.

Divelli answered them. They then stabbed him and tossed the office, without finding the money, which was found by the police later on hidden inside the copier.

The police in the small Arkansas town where they lived had few resources. Even the coroner was just a country doctor. The police claimed, with no supporting evidence and no knife in hand, that Divelli had been stabbed with a butcher knife. Since Gloria Divelli and her husband had often argued even in public, she was taken into custody and charged with his murder.

Ryker studied the reports, and realized that the knife wound was the wrong shape to be made by a butcher knife. The shape of the wound was more from a switch blade knife. Also, he could see no reason why Gloria would ransack her husband's office.

Ryker now turned his attention to Bloomberg and Dustman, and to their company Richmont. He felt that one of them was much more likely to be the murderer than Gloria might be.

One day Ryker followed Bloomberg to the FPL office and waited until he came out carrying a bag. Ryker came up close behind him and said, "Don't turn around. I have a gun pointed directly at your kidneys. Walk across the street at the corner and go into the park and into the restroom there."

Bloomberg did what he was told to do. Someone was in the restroom standing at the urinal, which Bloomberg saw as an advantage.

He turned suddenly and hit Ryker. The man at the urinal quickly zipped up his pants and disappeared.

Ryker had been lying when he said he had a gun, but he held his own in the fistfight, until he slipped on some water and fell. Bloomberg produced a switchblade, but Ryker was back on his feet. He was familiar with knife fights and fended off several swipes. Then Ryker caught Bloomberg's right hand and twisted his arm around to his back. The knife fell and Ryker kicked it into one of the stalls. Bloomberg was still holding his bag with his left hand.

Holding Bloomberg's arm high behind his back, Ryker said very coyly, "What's in the bag?"

"Money," replied Bloomberg.

"You came out of a women's charity. Do you change into women's clothes before going in? Are you some kind of queer cross-dresser so you can get lots of money from them? Do you rob them at knife point? How do you get them to give you lots of money?"

"They just give it to me."

"That sounds awfully suspicious. Why not a nice legal check? Why do they give money to a man? Shouldn't it be given to a woman?"

"No, because, I own the place."

"Is that so? Why don't we take that bag and your illegal switchblade down to the police department where they can ask more questions and get a warrant to search the FPL books?"

Ryker picked up the knife, and still holding Bloomberg's arm behind him, marched him to the nearby police station. The police took Bloomberg into custody. Ryker gave them the switchblade and said, "If you send this to the Little Rock lab, they will probably find traces of Divelli's blood on it, and you will have your real murderer. You might also want to audit the books of Richmont and the FPL."

The Little Rock lab confirmed that there were traces of Divelli's blood on the switchblade and that the shape matched the wound he had suffered.

"You're Honor," the Prosecutor said, "if I may interrupt the proceedings. Mr. Ryker Fleming has submitted new evidence proving Gloria Divelli to be innocent. The prosecution wishes to withdraw all charges against her."

"You are free to go, Mrs. Divelli," announced the Judge. "The jury is dismissed with the thanks of the Court."

The books of Divelli's firm, the Richmont firm, and the FPL were all audited. Then, as much as possible, the money was returned to the victims of the frauds.

Ryker took some time off for a short vacation and then returned to his office. He asked his secretary, Marty, "Did any new clients show up with interesting cases while I was gone?"

Marty handed him a few folders saying, "These are the only ones I felt would be worthy of your attention. Take a look, and see if you agree."

Hiding Out
By Howard Berg

Andrew decided to do some push-ups, but he could only do a few of them. There was a time he could do many more. Getting older was no fun. What upset him more was that he was on the run, and running and hiding from the police was easy, only when he was younger.

Now he was hiding from the Gang. The Gang had been his employer for decades, and there was no problem, until one of the boss's grandkids accused Andrew falsely of stealing money from the safe that was in the wall in their large condominium.

Why did this young punk say he saw Andrew fooling around with the lock on the safe? Andrew denied it quite strongly. It wasn't true, but they did not believe him. Some gratitude he felt, for the loyal years that he had put in for the group. Doing their bidding for any endeavor, including robbery, shootings, murdering's, intimidations, fraud, breaking into stores, and outright meanness, etc. was difficult, without all of his help over the many years.

One of the buddies from the group stopped by his apartment. He told Andrew that he should leave the city of Detroit as soon as possible, because he had heard if the money was not returned in a couple of days, they would seek to destroy him.

Andrew took the warning seriously. Within hours he had left town and headed by plane for the city of Los Angeles. At least he had some friends there. He used a false name for the airline tickets and was thankful for the years he had instructions on how to make false ID's.

He took a taxi when he landed and was not worried because he had a low profile in Los Angeles, and that was for an episode that took place more than eight years ago.

Unknown to him, as he exited the plane, a plainclothes officer was taking a look at some of the male passengers, and taking pictures of them as well. His department was looking for drug dealers from the San Francisco area and the Midwest who were hoping to increase their territory as Los Angeles had done.

Sure enough, later at the headquarters, one of the older detectives noticed Andrew's picture as a person to watch. He knew of Andrew from lineups, and felt that even at Andrew's age there was no good reason for him to be in Los Angeles. In checking later, they also noticed the lack of his real name on the passenger list.

Andrew's friend, Tom, was retired and lived by himself, so he was glad to see him and give him a place to stay. Andrew said to him, "Thanks, Tom, I should only be here for a few weeks. I'm going to look for an apartment." He then told his old friend why he had come to Los Angeles and all about the Gang and the situation that was false and why they had forced him to leave.

He took a series of walks in the next few days, and he noticed all the neat apartment buildings in the nearby blocks. He then realized this would be a good place to hide out for a few months.

At the end of his most recent walk, he noticed a police car in front of Tom's apartment building. It scared him. Perhaps they were looking into someone else in the building. To think things over he walked back a ways and went into a bar and restaurant on the corner and thought things over for a time.

After he calmed down, he went outside and returned to his friend's room. His friend confirmed that the police were looking for him. Something about using a false ticket on a plane trip, they thought.

Lordee, thought Andrew, just what he did not need. How would he explain the ticket amongst other things. Just what he needed--two big detective firms looking for him. How unlucky could one be?

The plainclothes policeman who had taken the pictures decided with his boss to give the info and pictures that were important to someone who was not in a police uniform, so as not to be seen by the man they sought. They gave all the info to a private detective named Ryker Fleming. They had used Fleming's skills many times to augment their investigations. It was one of a few folders that Ryker took a second look at.

Ryker decided to take the job of hunting this long time man of ill repute. His first step was to park his car a good block away and observe his friend's apartment building, to see if things were quiet.

The police who had been there before had the phone number, so after waiting a good two hours he called the man to see if Andrew had called or come back in. The man told Ryker to come up, since he had not seen Andrew in five days.

Ryker went up to the third floor carefully and found the apartment okay. He knocked on the door and was let in. He said to the man nicely, "Thank you for talking to me about this man. We just want to talk to him about his credentials when buying a ticket to fly across the country."

Tom seemed to understand, and explained that they were high school friends and had not seen each other in many years. He explained the gang connection to Ryker as much as he could, and why Andrew was trying to hide out in Los Angeles. He said to Ryker, "He is scared of the gang, and I imagine that is why he used fake ID so they could not follow him."

That made sense, Ryker thought. Tom told Ryker that Andrew did not want to tell him just where he was moving to only that it would be an apartment somewhere nearby. "There was a bar with a restaurant on the next corner that

Andrew liked," he told the detective, "And that is the only info I can give you that might help you."

Ryker thanked the man and said he appreciated the help. Also the man should know that a strong possibility existed that the gang would and could find out where Andrew flew to. If so, they might just come to his apartment! Little did he know how accurate his words were going to be.

When Ryker left, he thought Andrew might still show up if he was still watching the building. So he walked away to his car, then walked back and sat on a bench almost directly across from the apartment which was a bus stop and where a man and woman were usually seen waiting.

About 20 minutes later a car moved slowly within the traffic, and went around the block and slowed down again in front of the building. The next time it came back and stopped. Two men got out and the driver stayed in the car, with the motor running. Ryker could see the out-of-state license plate. He was curious more than anything that the men were moving quite swiftly into the building. And they came back out even faster, hopped into the car, and it zoomed away.

All that made him even more curious, so he went back up to the apartment. Door not locked, and Tom, to whom he had just talked to a few minutes earlier, was laying on his back on the living floor with his eyes wide open. Ryker knelt down and said, "What happened to you?"

Tom barely could whisper that the men were from the Detroit gang that had wanted Ralph. He barely could be heard when he said they did not believe him and that is why they shot him. No response after that, as his breathing and responses then ceased.

Ryker was disturbed greatly. He had been disturbed many times in his police and detective occupations, but when he saw civilians like Tom murdered for no good reason, it still stunned him. Lots of bad luck in life, he thought.

He would rest a minute and then call the police lieutenant who had been there earlier with his men who were looking for Andrew. He realized Tom had been telling the truth all along. Fine honest fellow, this Tom. Since the gang did this, it appeared that Andrew was the only one now in serious trouble.

The lieutenant arrived with a group of men and surveyed the situation. Ryker told him how he was watching the place. "It took a few minutes and I'm just impressed that they found Andrew's first spot upon arrival so fast and have traveled so far to apparently do away with him.

"If you can keep from reporting this murder here for 48 hours, we might be able to do damage to the notorious gang. I need to find Andrew so he can fill me in on any particulars. I think he now will do it. Not only because he is on the run from them, but also when I find him and tell him about Tom's death, he will help us. I am sure of that."

Later after the body was removed and the police detail left, Ryker went down toward the corner to the bar-restaurant and sat at a table to have an early   dinner. Sure enough, about 20 minutes later, Andrew walked in right by him. Realizing that Andrew did not know him, Ryker got up as Andrew went past him to the bar. So he got up and slowly went over next to him, and ordered dessert.

He said quietly to Andrew, "I know who you are, and I am on your side. The gang is in the area. They went to Tom's apartment and without results as to where you were, they shot him to death. I'm a private investigator who was initially looking for you just to ask questions about your fake airline ticket. Nothing more. But now we know why you did that and now we just want you to help us get the gang members who are here to do away with you. Eh?"

Andrew looked flabbergasted and for a moment could barely speak. "Give me your name again and let me see your ID," he mumbled. Ryker accommodated him and then when Andrew was a little more stable invited him back to the table.

Andrew ordered a small dinner and Ryker got dessert. Andrew said "It is funny that now the law is on my side. I'm not used to that."

Ryker said, "After what you've been through I suspect you now wish to slow down and take things very easy. Am I right?"

"Right on," Andrew said. "Here is my phone number and the location where I am staying. I will write it down for you. Now tell me how they found the city I fled to and roughly knew where I was. I suspect there must be a mole in the police department. What do you know about that?"

Ryker said he agreed with him, and was going to look into that strong possibility. He would let him know tomorrow. They agreed to meet for dinner again right there on tomorrow night.

Next morning Ryker stopped at the police station to talk with the lieutenant. The lieutenant said he already found who the snitch was because he himself realized the strong possibility of it being a factor. The discredited policeman who was the one who took the pictures of arriving passengers, was now being held for further facts and for his contacts. Fortunately, because Tom, who was killed, did not know where Andrew had moved to, the snitch and police did not know either.

Ryker thought, "Two plus two equals four." The gang may look at local bars and restaurants as he had done. So he called Andrew and told him right away to get ready and he would pick him up and explain later. He told him to wait in his room. He would come up and get him.

When he got there all looked well. He opened the lobby door and took a quick look behind him to see the street. There pulling up was the same car he had seen at Tom's place when that disaster had happened.

He ran up to Andrew's third floor apartment, and knocked hard to get him to open the door. He yelled "The gang car with three people just pulled up. Come'n right now. We will find the back door. Now!"

Andrew agreed quickly and they took off down the hall to the back stairs. Ryker brought out his 38 Colt piece and it felt good in his hand. As he started down with Andrew behind him, he heard and saw a gang member coming up. "Stop right there, fella," he yelled down to him. The man reached behind him for his weapon, and as he brought it out, Ryker felled him with a fast shot to his chest.

They started down the stairwell, got a few steps, and then they heard someone in the hallway calling from above for his friend. Ryker said "Wait here," and with his pistol drawn walked slowly back up the stairs to see if the fellow was at Andrew's door. That would mean more trouble indeed. And the man he saw at Tom's door entered it, came right out, and looked both ways until he saw Ryker. He started to go under his jacket to get his shoulder gun, but Ryker fired first.

This left just the driver, so Ryker called his buddy at the station and told him what happened and to not use a siren, but to arrest the driver. He walked down the stairs to where Andrew was waiting and they went down all the way and walked almost to the front.

Again Ryker said, "Wait here." Knowing that the driver of the car was still there, he wanted to hold him until police arrived. He walked down the sidewalk, opened the door, and said to the youthful driver that he could not park there as the sign said for deliveries only in that area. The driver looked confused, but he had no weapon showing and was quite young, so Ryker got in, pulled out his weapon and said to the driver he was under arrest. The police arrived a few minutes later.

Before the police took the youth away, Ryker went around the corner to get Andrew and took him to the police wagon to look at the arrested fellow. After a short look, Andrew told Ryker that it was the young grandson of their leader and that he was the instigator of all this trouble with his lies. He explained it carefully to Ryker.

The young man, now in handcuffs, heard all this, and his head drooped noticeably.

Justified Injustice
By Kent Humpal

"Thanks boss, I can use the time away from the office and phone. I wrote a brief description of the cases and the clients. There are some sites listed on the Internet if you need more background. Bye! See you tomorrow." Marty closed the door as she left.

Ryker was looking over the cases while sitting on his elevated deck sipping Pinot Noir. Two discarded folders sat on the floor. He had decided on a case, but wondered if he was capable and willing. It involved an art theft and recovery, and it went back to the Warsaw Ghetto uprising. Some of his grandparents cousins had died there and later in the Death Camps. It was close to home.

His grandparents had escaped Europe after Kristallnacht, and done well for themselves. His father and uncles had served in World War II, and Ryker remembered the stories of his dad and uncles. He'd take the case, if only to honor his family.

"Marty, can you set up a meeting with Jonas Rossman and his sister Rosina Rossman

Gwertzen. I need to meet them before I take this case. It has some international features and legal questions," was Ryker's explanation.

Marty ushered in two people, accompanied by the wife or husband. "Thank you for coming in. My name is Ryker and I'm interested in your case. Can we talk candidly about your interest in the case?"

"My name is Jonas Rossman. This is my sister Rossina Gwertzen, my wife, Helenna, and my brother-in-law, Rudolph Gwertzen. We would like to recover a painting stolen from our family, specifically from our grandparents by the Nazis in World War II."

"How did you become aware of this painting?" asked Ryker. "Excuse me, may I record our conversation? It is considered confidential, of course, especially if you become my client. Otherwise I will give it to you to keep or dispose of as you wish, in case you don't use my services."

"My sister was responsible for that. Sina, why don't you take over?"

"Yes, our grandfather, Guenter Rossman, was Austrian in a prominent Jewish family involved in banking, although he was into art as both a collector and dealer/agent. He represented many of the Art Nouveau painters of the 1920's and 1930s.

One of his artists was a young Austrian impressionist named Röetger Landeburg. He was becoming popular and his work was selling, nothing spectacular, but selling constantly.

He was becoming known by collectors. He died of typhus while traveling, leaving behind several paintings in my grandfather's gallery. His family claimed most of his work, but gave my family a painting for our friendship and sponsorship of their son. It was a late production and it had never been displayed.

"With his death, as often happens, Landeburg's paintings went up in value. When the Nazis took over Austria, our grandparents went to Poland. They had to leave everything behind. They moved into a family home, hoping to get to Portugal eventually. When the Germans moved in they gave up hope of getting things out of Austria."

"Yes, I'm aware of that. My family came from there. How did you know of the painting's reappearance?" questioned Ryker.

"Well, our parents were sent to Canada. Our grandmother was Austria-Czech and got visas from a Czech official. Anyway, the story was passed down with a catalog from the gallery showing the painting. None of us liked it, but it's one of the few things left of our family's inheritance."

"I am a docent for a local museum and a brochure came in from an auction house and there was our painting staring at me. Listed by Röetger, date and place, but not who the seller was or its value. It is not to our taste, but it was ours, and our family wants it back. We think by international law it should be returned to us."

"I assume you have contacted the auction house and filed a claim through the proper channels?" queried Ryker.

"Yes, they're semi-cooperative, but they won't release the name of the seller--just a representative and an attorney. We seem to be at a stalemate," answered Jonas Rossman.

"There is another problem, though. The auction house claims it has been taken from the workshop of the authenticator restorer with whom they contract. He is highly regarded and well considered by other galleries. "We want it back. It needs to be recovered and authenticated again," stated Jonas.

"You already know my fees and have agreed to finance any additional costs. I will take the case and will contact the auction gallery to see if they will cooperate. They may be willing to share the fees, even if they or their client loose custody of the painting."

The next several weeks Ryker was in and out of the office. He had given some of his less interesting cases to subordinates and sent a few clients to other agencies that often worked with him.

Usually a close confident, Marty was getting frustrated and bothered by not being able to answer client inquiries. "Marty, will you please call up the Rossman- 2 people and have them come into the office two days from now. What is that, Thursday? That's fine. The gallery will be ready by then."

"Good afternoon. I thank you for heeding my pleas. No outsiders or attorneys--only family. First, we have found and recovered the painting. It was being held at the auction gallery," explained Ryker.

"Why then don't we have control? It's ours, isn't it?" asked Rossina Gwertzen.

"Well, there were some things you didn't disclose. It made negotiations somewhat unusual and involved."

"What do you mean? Sina and I told you everything!"

"Yes, except for the family rumors, and tales handed down at dinners and get togethers. Right?" inquired Ryker.

"Well, yes, but those were just tales, you know, like Great Aunt Emeline was an attendant for the Queen of Romania, or Cousin Antoine was a staff officer for Bismarck. Probably some truth, but very exaggerated."

"Well, it's good you didn't like the painting because the authenticator found a better one underneath it. The gentleman is a colleague and we have worked together several times. With your permission, he will restore the original. Of course, that will destroy the Landeburg painting."

"But won't the gallery and the people that had it fight that? They will lose money and the painting." Jonas questioned.

"Ah! This is where discretion and cooperation come about. Let me tell you a story and how this can be resolved, if you agree."

"In late 1944, a squad of the 82nd airborne was sweeping through Bavaria. They were liberating a village when they came across a large villa on a lake. The locals said it was one of Goering's retreats. The team, of course, decided to search it. Looking for souvenirs, the sergeant snatched this painting off the floor, stuck it in his backpack, and shipped it home in his footlocker. About a year ago his family was cleaning out the basement and found it wrapped in an army shirt at the bottom of the locker. You can guess the rest."

"But what is your solution? How does this work to everyone's acceptance?" asked Rossina.

"That depends on your agreement. This is what I, and the other involved parties have come up with. The gallery and the family have agreed to donate the painting to a museum in Vienna for recovered artwork. The gallery and the soldier's family will receive recognition and publicity for a good deed. Your family will also be noted as donors."

"But the painting—it can't be both here and there. How does that happen?" again asked Rossina.

"Here is where the discretion and secrecy sets in. The restorer was, and is, one of the finest duplicators in the art world. In truth, he was a forger for years, working out of the Philippines. Much of his work is hanging on the walls of oligarchs, billionaires, and Middle Eastern rulers, who think they have the real thing. Even a few museums have them. The present age recognizes his abilities and displays his work on their walls labelled as reproductions. If you wish, you can award the family and gallery with a donation."

The family went into another room to discuss the situation. Coming out, Jonas Rossman stepped forward. "We all agree with the actions and we will contact the others involved. Thank you for the innovative solution. It may well become another family rumor."

"Your original landscape will be delivered by courier. It's a beautiful work, according to my friend.

"Marty will show you out."

Twenty minutes later Ryker stepped out of his office. "Marty, what have you got for me?"

Entangled
By Virginia Braxton

Ryker was in a foul mood. He was catching up on his insurance work, which he hated, but it paid the rent and staff salaries. He was almost shouting to Marty. "What kind of dumb ass is this guy? He claims workmen's comp for an injury that will keep him in a wheelchair for the rest of his life, and then, in broad daylight, he climbs up a ladder and starts shingling his roof! There's no artistry or intelligence in that! I don't like the insurance companies, for that's just stupid fraud!"

He appeared to be willing to go on this way for the next hour, so Marty, who was the only person in the office with him that day, said his insurance work paid the bills, and she was going to take her lunch and eat it in the park across the street. She settled in her favorite spot and calmed down as she finished her sandwich. The spring sun felt good on her skin, and she was almost asleep when she felt a touch on her knee.

She opened her eyes to see a child with red hair and enormous brown eyes staring up at her.

"Mama," the child said.

Marty judged the little girl to be about 18 months old, and she looked around for a responsible adult who might claim her. In the distance, she could see a figure slumped on a bench, but it ignored them. Bending a bit to take the child's hand, she walked over to the slumped figure.

"Biddie, Biddie," cried the child and tried to climb on the woman's lap, but Marty pulled her away. As Ryker's colleague, she had seen enough dead people to recognize death, even when they were fresh and with no obvious cause.

She reached for her phone. Some time ago, Ryker had set up a distress signal on her phone that she could activate with one button. She had thought it was silly, but now she pushed the button.

She turned the child's back to the body and stepped slightly away from it, as she waited for Ryker. She was surprised at how quickly she saw him loping toward her.

"What happened? Are you okay?" And his tone was softening. "Who's this?" gesturing toward the child.

"I don't know. She just came up to me and took me to her," Marty, said, pointing to the woman's body.

"I'll call the police," said Ryker punching buttons, "And," he continued into the phone, "in addition to Homicide for the unexplained death, we'll need Child Protective Services, because there's a toddler here who doesn't seem to have an attached adult."

Ryker put his jacket around Marty and the child, who were both beginning to shake, and spoke   soothingly to them while he waited for reinforcements. When the police arrived, he was pleased to see "Mack" McCarthy, a colleague from his FBI days, was leading the team. Mack came straight to Ryker.

"Hello, Ryker," he said. "What's the story?"

"All I know," replied Ryker, "is that my office manager, Marty, here, was eating her lunch in the park, when this child came up to her. Marty looked around for an attending adult and found the body over there. She called me for help—and I called you. I'll let her tell you herself."

Just then, Mack spotted a tall woman in plain clothes with a diaper bag slung over her shoulder striding toward them. "Good," he said, "C.P.S. sent Sheila. She's really good. Used to be in homicide, but now is flourishing in C.P.S."

He introduced the tall woman as Sheila Bloomfield. Sheila immediately focused on the child, smiling, and cooing a bit while she held out her arms. The child hesitated a moment and then went to her.

"Ooof!" Sheila exclaimed sniffing the child! "This one needs a clean diaper." She strode over to the tent where the crime scene team was working and evicted all but one of the technicians. "So," she said, "this young lady can have some privacy."

Marty had finished telling Mack the little she knew about what had happened, by the time Sheila returned carrying a transformed child. The grime had been washed off, and her clothes were fresh, and she was clutching a blanket.

Sheila said, "This child has been well cared for and, as far as I can tell, has not been abused or   physically hurt. Of course, she'll need a more   thorough medical examination.

"So I'm taking her to the University's pediatric hospital. We've opened a clinic especially for children who have been traumatized and/or abused. Among other things, the clinic has the fastest turnaround on DNA tests in the state. I've got all the necessary samples and have left a set with your technicians. So Girl Doe and I are off now."

"No!" exclaimed Ryker. "You mustn't call her 'Girl Doe!' 'Doe' is for dead people and she's not dead!" He paused. "Let's see. She's beautiful. We should call her Bella."

"All right," said Sheila, "Bella she'll be until we find out her real name. And you, Ryker, are now her godfather."

"Can I come visit her?" Ryker asked, and on being assured that Bella would be at the hospital for at least 24 hours, nodded and turned his attention to Marty.

"Look, I don't think you should be alone tonight. Will it be my place or yours?"

"I really want to be home, now," said Marty, so they made a quick stop at the office and headed to her place.

The next morning Marty woke up to the fragrance of coffee. She stumbled into the kitchen and found a huge teddy bear sitting at her counter. She blinked, swallowed some coffee, and looked again. The bear was still there.

She was still looking at it when Ryker came in.

"Isn't it great?" he asked. "I had Tony drop it off last night. It's for Bella."

"Hmm," said Marty as she envisioned her office filling up with toys for Bella and even some useful things like a playpen and a changing table.

"Don't worry. Sheila says I can visit Bella, so I'm taking the bear with me when I go. Do you want to come?"

When Ryker, Marty, and The Bear, arrived at the hospital they were told that Bella was in the middle of a session with the linguist and they must wait to talk to her.

While they were waiting, Sheila came to them. "The good news is that the doctors confirmed that Bella has been well cared for and not abused in any way they can detect. The puzzling news is that our rapid DNA test shows she has no biological relationship to the woman she was found with."

"A babysitter?" hazarded Ryker, "And what's the linguist doing with her anyway?"

"Trying to determine what language she's used to hearing. We know she spoke to Marty, but she has stopped talking. Her language might give us a clue. There've been no missing children reports that fit her.

"Ahh. We can go in now," Sheila said, as she opened the door.

Proudly bearing The Bear before him and peaking over it's shoulder, Ryker entered the room saying, "Look Bella! Look who's here to see you!"

Bella wailed and then buried her head in the linguist's lap.

"Well, that didn't go over too well," said a crest fallen Ryker.

"Ryker put The Bear on the floor, and spoke soothingly to Bella," instructed Sheila. "When she lifts her head, make The Bear play peek-a-boo."

Finally, Bella reached out to touch The Bear, and, feeling its texture, grabbed it with both hands.

Ryker grinned.

Ryker and Marty were outside the hospital, when Ryker spotted Mack coming towards them. The two men exchanged greetings.

Mack said, "We're running the corpse's fingerprints through Interpol, but no match has been made yet. The papers she had on her said she was Bridget Casey, but they were extremely good forgeries—among the best I've seen. She may have been a courier. Autopsy's not finished yet.

"Because Bella was with the corpse and there's no missing child report yet, we're thinking there may be a connection to the black market in babies." His tone deepened. "The children are just commodities, sold to people who don't have the patience to jump through the hoops that the legitimate agencies, especially the international ones, require! I'd rather deal with drug dealers." He paused for a moment to control himself.

"Bella may be in danger. She's a valuable commodity and they don't like business losses."

"Look, Mack," said Ryker, "I'm taking Bella on as a client, in my capacities both as a private investigator and as a lawyer. I'm still a member of the bar, you know, even though I'm not actively practicing law. I can represent her whenever she needs legal representation."

"I'll keep that in mind," responded Mack, "It might be useful."

A few days later Marty and Sheila were at the hospital visiting Bella. They had decided to walk around the hospital grounds so that Bella could get some fresh air, but as Bella refused to be parted from The Bear, they put Bear in a borrowed wheelchair, and Bella sat on his lap.

They were near the end of their walk, when a man jumped out from the bushes brandishing a hypodermic needle and aiming it at Bella. Sheila tackled the assailant, bringing him down so forcefully he cracked his head and passed out. At the same time, Marty grabbed Bella and the hypo went into Bear's head. Hospital Security came running, restraining the assailant, and carting him off to have his head treated. Bella wailed, "Bear hurt! Bear hurt!"

"She's talking! She's talking!," Sheila crowed. Then she ordered, "Bag the hypo, it's evidence. I'm calling Mack and Ryker."

By the time they arrived, things were quieter. Bella was saying "Bear has ouch," while tenderly putting a Band Aid on his head.

Mack surveyed the scene. "Sheila, that cross on the chain around Bella's neck. Has she always had it?"

"Yes," replied Sheila. "She had it when we found her. I didn't want to take away the only thing she had, so we put it back on after the technician had thoroughly processed it. I put that all in the report."

Mack looked thoughtful. "Wait inside for me. I have to get something."

When Mack returned, he handed a small box to Sheila and said, "Here, put this on Bella, and give me the cross she's wearing."

"But, Bella's cross is a Celtic silver cross and this one is gold and a different shape."

"Botonée cross. Yes, that's the point," said Mack. "No one can mistake one for the other. I'm hoping the obvious difference will protect Bella. I'll take the   original cross to the lab to be examined with equipment the field technician didn't have."

Ryker held Bella while Mack exchanged the crosses. "Shouldn't we pray or something," Ryker asked. "Mack, you go to church. Can you?"

Mack gathered himself and resting his hand gently on Bella's head, prayed, "Our Father, protect this wee girl and help us also to protect and care for her. Let her grow up in the certainty that she is loved by You and by us. Amen."

Several days passed before Mack stopped by Ryker's office, which was beginning to resemble a child care center.

Mack settled into the comfortable chair Ryker used for relaxing, and announced, "The autopsy on Jane Doe, aka Bridget, was a surprise. It determined that she died a natural death, some kind of heart anomaly. She probably didn't know she had it, but it was a time bomb that happened to go off while she was there in the park.

"While we still have not had a missing child report corresponding to Bella, we're making progress.

"We now have a number of pieces of evidence pointing to the Irish Republic in connection with the baby black market. Bella's DNA from both parents shows she has multiple, but distant cousins in Ireland.

"The clothes she was wearing were made by nuns and sold to raise money for the order at only one shop in Belfast. Oddly, these particular nuns have not yet discovered the Internet.

"The Celtic Cross she was wearing was handmade and probably came from a shop a few doors from the one that sold the clothes.

"Neither the Irish police nor Interpol have any previous records on the assailant, who has steadfastly refused to say more than 'yes,' 'no,' and 'I don't know,' but yesterday when he stubbed his toe, he swore in Gaelic.

"So this seems more than a coincidence and we're putting lots more resources into the investigation in Ireland. I hope we catch the bastards!"

"As you know, Sheila has found a couple as foster and possible adoptive parents. They were formerly in law enforcement, so they understand Bella's circumstances. I hear you and Bella visited them this week."

"Yes," Ryker responded, "They're good people. And they've promised to let me and Marty visit Bella regularly. Did you know that Bella has a name for me now?"

"What is it?" queried Mack.

"Well," replied Ryker flushing slightly, it's 'Goppa.' Baby talk, but she clearly has attached it to me and no one else."

Section Two
Individual Stories

Numerous Creative Writing Stories are published by writers in this book each day. They are listed below for you to read.

Apache Doings
By Howard Berg

The name of the chief scout is Gettia. He has Apache blood because his Apache mother married an Arizona settler, and she was loyal to him when they were farming or when they were prospecting. They had a boy, Gettia, who was eight years old when an Apache raiding party attacked their farm.

The mother and father were slain in the Apache raid, and the raiders took the boy with them. He was living with them until he was about 18 years old, and then he went to the village overseen by the U.S. First Cavalry in Salisbury.

It was about 12 miles away. He took different jobs for a few months to survive. The head of the First Cavalry found out about him and he offered Gettia a job as one of his scouts, because of his ability to speak the Apache language.

Over the next 10 years, he became head chief of about seven total scouts. It turned out quite well for Gettia as he became chief scout for the cavalry and taught the leading officer Stevens all he knew about the Apaches.

Colonel Stevens took him under his wing and taught Gettia much that he needed to know about his new surroundings. Gettia remembered much from his early years, so he turned out to be of superb help in dealing with the Apache people.

Both the domestic tribes who were settled in one direction as a group and doing some good degree of farming down south of Salisbury, and those tribes that were still at periodic war with the people in and near Salisbury. This much tougher and meaner group was based about 18 miles north of Salisbury.

This is how Gettia explained who he was and how he was now living on the second floor of the only   hotel in town. Gettia had explained it this way to the lady and her father who had come up to see Gettia as the father had just bought the small restaurant in town and wanted to know more about the community.

They were hoping to walk and ride around near the town before the sun became too strong in the coming weeks. So in the meanwhile it was   comfortable in the shade of the room, while they talked more about the village.

They left after about an hour's conversation and in a few minutes another guest arrived and knocked lightly on the door. It was Colonel Stevens with two of his troopers who also came in. Colonel Stevens was very excited.

"Gettia, guess what I found out about that large mountain north of here, over into the northeast. The one they call Whiteface. There is a small opening on the other side that leads inside to a fabulous gold mine, from 45 years ago, when it was active. And it has been unknown until now."

"I know the mountain quite well, but never was on the east side," answered Gettia. "Trouble is, it's near that very tough group of Apaches who are in the vicinity."

They finally decided to take an investigative trip with 12 troopers, Gettia, and the colonel.

Also they brought some meat and food to give to this group of Apaches near the mountain.

It took three days to get to the tribe and meet with their leaders. The tribe leaders seemed indifferent, but wanted them to go to the mountain there, and be done in a week, and then leave. They were happy about the food that was left for them.

The Apache leader's name was Redondo and his son-in -law, whom Gettia remembered from growing up with him, was called Teconal. Teconal smiled at Gettia but did not talk with him.

The group finally traveled to the other side of the mountain which they could see all the way from the village. It was about six miles away and they searched for the small opening about one quarter of the way up the east side of the mountain. They searched for about four hours. Once found, they entered with torches and spent the next morning looking around the vast interior. They saw some shovels and tools from long-ago prospecting. The veins on the walls looked stunning in their glowing appearance.

With no waste of time, Gettia and the colonel got right to work and were overjoyed. Gettia sent two of the newer troopers to watch at the opening of the cave and told them to walk slowly, and if they could, manage to keep watch on the Apache village from afar. Gettia wanted a warning in case the Apaches looked like they are coming up the mountain on their side.

Unknown to him, these two new freshman troopers were about to cause much trouble. The taller one of them is Alex and the short one is Walter. They transversed the mountain circumference easily as it is cool in the shade of the brush and trees and they sneaked up and from afar to watch the village. The sun is beginning to cause some warmth on their faces.

They see a couple of young female Apache girls playing near the trees after a while. Going wacky, they walk down the slope further, approach them, make nice to them, and get carried away. Alex, after a while starts kissing the one female, and she pulls him to her.

But, there is difficulty shortly after that, and after a few moments she pushes Alex aside and runs towards her village swiftly. Both troopers look at each other and then agree to not follow. They decide to return to the cave instead.

On the way back they are only halfway home when Walter, who is in front, hears a grunt from his buddy and when he turns around he sees Alex lying flat down with an arrow in his back. A crimson color liquid is spreading out on his jacket. He grabs his buddy's rifle from his hands and starts running as fast as he can off the path through the trees to the cave. More than one arrow goes whizzing by.

Walter makes it and yells for help as he approaches the mouth of the cave. Scout Gettia comes out with Colonel Stevens, and Walter tells him what has happened, leaving nothing out.

Colonel Stevens turns around and yells "Men, grab your rifles and get out here." They come and he tells them to form up behind him. A few seconds later a dozen Apaches approach slowly up the slope to the cave's mouth.

Gettia speaks to them, greeting them carefully. Chief Redondo says, "Two of your troopers assaulted two of our young women. We want them! Now."

Gettia tells him that the two troopers made a mistake in talking to the women. No harm was done. But you already have killed the one who touched the woman. No harm was done. The one who returned here will be punished by our officers.

The chief of the Apaches said quietly to Gettia, "We shall see." Then he turned and took his men away.

Gettia conferred with the Colonel. Fortunately, the troopers had the latest rifles, the Winchester model 50S, which carried a large, easily loaded magazine, and was exceptionally accurate. While the Apaches had rifles, they had no ammunition.

The Colonel and Gettia selected the trooper who was the oldest and most experienced and within 10 minutes sent him to follow the Barker creek down to Salisbury for extra troopers to come and have them travel up the creek to meet them; and all of the rest of the outfit would follow along the creek on the east side, as it got wider as the miles grew for easier defense.

Within an hour, the Colonel and Gettia had the squad ready to go. And they did, rifles loaded and eyes and ears at top peak as they went down the mountain to the creek and walked their horses and rode them when the view was good. Going forward and looking across the water at the same time they had two men a few yards behind the rest to listen for Apaches who might be following on their trail.

With about three hours daylight left, it was good they picked the east bank because the brush was less and easier to ride or walk. One of the troopers saw movement across the creek and within seconds about eight Apaches yelling and screaming entered the creek and let loose with arrows. Colonel Stevens told the men to hold their fire until the Indians were closer. One man held four horses and the rest kneeled down behind bushes and slowly but accurately got rounds off at the attackers.

The men had been trained for just such an episode and with patience and accuracy the rifles sounded off loudly and the eight Apaches wen t down with certainty. A few arrows landed nearby but caused no injuries.

The colonel got the men remounted and headed down along the creek further. Gettia told the Colonel he felt the Apaches would cross the creek during the night and try a surprise attack when the troopers might be resting, or tomorrow in daylight, from behind.

Gettia had spent some important time with most of these men over the years and had explained to them how quiet and slow in moving the Apaches were as they approached to conquer an enemy. So he literally placed a man with a rifle in front of the troop when night fell and they rested and one man behind the troop as they slept. Both guards were in a location under bushes that were thick and good for cover. They each had a whistle and would sound it if the Apaches approached. After two or three hours other men would take their places.

Things worked out well and the whole troop returned to Salisbury. Gettia talked the next day with Colonel Stevens and suggested that they take about six Apaches from the domesticated group south of Salisbury with them next time and try to placate the Apaches up north that were still upset with the Cavalry. Stevens thought that would be a good approach.

The ounces of precious metals that they had garnered in those few hours required some kind of further trade of goods and words with the angry Apaches up north.

Surely at that moment it seemed like a great idea.

Shotgun Alley
By Howard Berg

Ronald had been out of prison for 18 months. He did not think anything could be worse than prison. He was quite bored and did not like his job as he had a hard time making money for rent and food. But no one had a good paying job for an ex-convict, especially in 1952. His girlfriend made breakfast for them every morning and paid most of the rent for the apartment.

His job was making stupid cardboard boxes. Sometimes little boxes and sometimes larger ones. But still, he needed more money.

He was out strolling trying to walk off the heat, when he noticed a small building down the street from where he worked. It was small and squat, built like a tank. It was a local branch of R&R Banking, constructed like a temple. It seemed to be calling out to him.

While he did not have an account there, he went in to observe the teller. He noticed that the tellers usually had a lot of cash in each drawer. He never had used guns, so he purchased a short shotgun the next day. He went to a skeet field to practice shooting and handling it.

He knew from newspaper reports that pistols scared the tellers so much that they froze and could not follow orders to hand over money. He knew that also from the discussions he had with other prisoners when he was in that horrible jail.

His idea was to make a box for the shotgun, show the end of the gun to the teller, and in a nice manner ask her for all the money in her drawers. He then made a box for the shotgun, which he surrounded with brown paper. He put the short box under his arm with the use of a strap, so he could just lift it a little out of the box so one could see it. He made another box a size that would hold a small loaf of bread. He would have the teller put the money in the bread box when he slid it to her.

The following Tuesday he went to the bank in the late afternoon. Just before entering, he put a black eye patch over one eye. There was only one other customer. There was only one teller. He walked over and said politely to the teller, "I have a shotgun ready to fire in this box under my arm. Be smart and intelligent and put all your cash into this smaller box that I am giving you."

Her eyes widened noticeably as he lifted the shotgun out of the box about two inches. She did as told. He walked casually out the door, then once through the doors, walked faster to his mini-factory seven doorways down the block. He went to his bench and put the packaged gun and box of money on his shelf near his tools. Other workers were busy and never looked at him. One big plus for employees was the ability to take a few minutes each shift to run local errands.

The following week he added a false mustache to his appearance. He then quit his job. He was convinced it was smart to stick with small banks. It worked nicely for three more weeks. When he could not find any more small banks, he bought a small car and went to the next city about 25 miles south of where he worked. He found a small bank right away.

He left his car two miles away from the first small bank he found. He found it best to check carefully these banks in the suburbs. Check that they had adjacent stores, whether a grocery store, drug store, library, department store, or any store where he would blend in, instead of running down the street during his get-away and drawing attention. It was another factor he must look at, he thought, as he ambled onward to the bank.

In the following weeks he added a false beard to his appearance. Small beard, but it stayed on. He waited till very late in the day when only one or two customers were inside. That was very important, as it was risky if too many customers were in there. The shotgun was wrapped in new paper every week. He always said, "Thank you very much" to the teller and walked out of each bank to a location previously selected.

He took a break and made it his new job to find where the small banks were located. There seemed to be at most two or three in most towns. So he moved slowly across the state.

He was about $64,000 ahead now. Stunning, he thought. Perhaps he should retire. He did not want to get caught.

"Wake up! Wake up! You're dreaming," the loud voice boomed. "You've been squirming and twisting and yelling, 'Too many people in here!' What kind of nonsense are you talking about? Wake up, wake up! Are you all right? Are you okay?"

His girlfriend was quite disturbed and upset. Ronald had difficult moments realizing he had been dreaming. Dreaming was so realistic that now he was quite happy because he knew just what he would do.

He spoke in a whisper and said to her that he would go back to the box company to work, but he would look for a new job. He had learned his lesson. He hadn't grown up. He was finally more mature and had found his destiny.

Grocery Carts
By Howard Berg

Henry went out onto the porch of his condo, and put his feet up on the railing. He liked to relax this way after sweeping the porch and the sidewalk in front of his place.

But now his nice view was disturbed. As he gazed across the lawn his entire attention was drawn to a long line of grocery carts that had been interlocked and placed intentionally across the street. This was not the first time this had been done. It wasn't the ,second or even the third time this grocery cart obstruction had been constructed. As a matter of fact this stunt had been performed every night for more than a week!

To the left and to the right of his condo, the other condos and apartments stretched about half a mile on both sides. He marveled at how wise it was to have bought this property about ten years ago. The view was still first rate. Rolling terrain of the golf course stretched almost as far as he could see in both the left and right directions. It showed the shallow terrain of a few of the back nine holes. Rolling hills and lovely grass that was well taken care of with regularity. A view that Henry really cherished!

But now, his perfect view was disturbed by empty grocery carts left right across from his condo. A whole line of them on the sidewalk across the street paralleling the short barbed wire fence of the golf course. The grocery store was just down the street about a half mile away. It was one of those big chain stores that are open 24 hours a day. Over the ten years that Henry had owned his condo and appreciated his view, it was not uncommon that on many mornings he would see the occasional cart left helter-skelter along the fence. But until recently he could expect that the store would send someone down to retrieve those "lost" carts by mid-morning.

About six weeks ago as it was getting just past dusk, he had seen a man pushing one of those grocery store carts and stopping across from Henry's house with it. The man retrieved a small package out of the cart and walked directly away to his condo, quite a few doors down.

Henry got up, walked out to the sidewalk, and saw the man disappear into the condo complex. Henry was not exactly sure which unit was his because it was too dark, and the evening shadows had already consumed part of the structure. The abandoned cart remained where it had been left for two whole days.

Perplexed by the abandoned shopping cart, on the third day and in broad daylight, Henry went across the street and pushed the cart down to approximately where he had seen the man cross the street and enter the complex. By the next morning or two mornings later, the same cart was back once again across the street from Henry, obstructing his view.

Henry was perplexed to say the least. What is going on with this guy? Is he lazy? Does he think we are saps down this way? Why does he not leave the carts in front of his apartment? Henry did ask at the grocery store, and he had seen them pick up two carts last week. The staff said it was a recurring problem and some people used them and normally did return them the next day or so.

This went on for about six weeks. A cart would be left during the night somewhat close to or exactly across from Henry. Henry would in broad daylight the next day push it back many yards to where the man lived.

The final straw happened when three grocery carts were left across from Henry when he awoke one morning. The following day he walked down to the distant area where he had often left them, found one man outside working on his small lawn, and asked him if he knew about the carts.

The man immediately got agitated and knew which fellow was doing it and he told Henry that he and some of his neighbors some months ago had complained to the man. He even told Henry which apartment the man lived in. He did not know or see that the man was now leaving them in front of Henry's place. He wished Henry well and warned him the man was difficult to deal with.

Henry left an enveloped letter in the man's mailbox asking him to stop by for a chat. About a week later the man knocked on Henry's front door. Henry welcomed him in and after introducing himself, he suggested that they sit on the front porch. The man agreed, adjusting his holstered pistol as he eased himself into the deck chair, giving Henry just a moment's hesitation when he noticed the firearm.

Henry asked, "Why are you leaving those carts in front of my house instead of in front of your home?"

"Because the grocery store will see them faster in front of your place or close to it, than in my location!"

Henry told him he could not believe that, and why did he take them and then leave the carts to begin with? The man stood up, loosened his pistol a tiny bit in the holster, and said it was none of Henry's damn business. Henry was a little bit stunned.

He decided he should alert some authority about this man. He talked to neighbors on each side of him. Then he walked down and talked to the man who gave him the exact address of the object of their   concern.

Most of the eight individuals who he talked to were members of the golf course across the street, so they all decided to meet for lunch on the upcoming Saturday in a meeting room at the golf course main building. The get together went well as all of them were upset because their view from their homes was being ruined over a very preventable situation. They hammered out a one page summary of what they all had witnessed happening over the last three months. They then each signed the document and the one member of the group who was a retired policeman volunteered to take it directly to the local police station.

Little changed except the weather. Carts were left either in front of Henry's location or down at the other site. One morning there were even two carts left. However on the eve of Thanksgiving, something changed.

Thanksgiving morning the group from down the street walked over and approached Henry who was sitting on his porch drinking coffee and reading the *New York Times*.

In stuttering haltering sentences, with voices filled with emotion, they explained that just before midnight, the man leaving the carts shoved a cart out into the street trying to hit a passing car. The driver swerved to miss the cart, hitting the man who had accidently taken a step into the road, while generating speed in his attempt to thrust the cart into the car. An ambulance and police car, lights flashing and sirens blaring came screeching onto the scene—even hitting two of the neglected grocery carts that had been accumulating near the fence.

The man, pistol still strapped to his side, was tossed into the air from the impact with the car, landing in one of the discarded grocery carts. He did not survive. Later that day, Henry and his neighbors   quietly returned the grocery carts back to the store where they belonged.

Ruthie's Father
By Howard Berg

Monte could not believe it. All he had to do when throwing the dice in the casino was to keep his throwing hand no higher than six or seven inches above the table. He had never played craps before. But Alex, a friend of his who lived across the street, had talked him into going along to the casino so Monte could learn the game.

The casino was a little over an hour away by bus, so they went together. Monte learned the rules fast. Like chess, the rules are quite simple, but it takes a much longer time to be successful at either game.

Monte had been a little hesitant to go. Alex was much older than him and came from a much wealthier family than Monte's. Alex was finishing college with a job pending. Monte was just going to be starting college if his parents could afford the cost.

Money was scarce after the war. 1949 was a tough year to get a job or earn any significant money, and Monte's father was still hobbling from a severe war wound he had received when he stormed the cliffs of Normandy.

On that first night they went together, Monte won a few hundred dollars and Alex lost many more times than that. What Monte noticed was that when the dice were pushed to him for his turn, Monte made sure that both the dice had the number 4 showing upright.

He didn't know why he did that and why he kept his hand low, very low, when he threw the dice to the other end of the table. It was then that he noticed he made most of his wins and money, as little as it was.

Alex did not notice that approach at all until the next day when he called Monte, because he had realized that Monte had won. No matter how little, but Monte had won—so he asked Monte, implored him, to explain just how he had done it.

As a result, they again went to the casino about two weeks later. Monte only had told Alex about keeping his throwing hand low above the felt table and betting hardly at all until it was his turn to throw the dice. So Monte was patient, but Alex was not patient, was betting, and was losing steadily. When Monte got his turn to roll the dice, Alex doubled up and got his money back. Simply doubling up almost on every new roll of Monte's.

Monte did his routine of turning the dice so that the number four showed on each of the dice. Then he threw five point numbers and made each point, hitting the established number without throwing a 7 and he kept the dice for 24 minutes, lots of time holding his turn.

Monte had over $800 in his rack. Alex, in the meantime, got all of his money back as he doubled up on Monte's roll for the session. He had over $2,200 in front of him and was ecstatic. All of the dozen people around the table applauded loudly for the great hand and were full of cheers and nice comments as well.

Alex wanted to leave right away, as he was a little stunned and wanted to think it over. He was very happy as he had been a loser until Monte got hold of the dice. Monte wanted to be shooter at least one more time, but Alex pleaded with him, so they left a few minutes later.

Later in the week Monte's new girlfriend, Ruthie, called him. She wanted to go and see a movie and later get some ice cream. Monte could barely restrain himself until they had the ice cream in front of them, and then he told her of his good luck at the casino table.

"I do not know how the game is played," she politely answered, "Tell me more!"

He told her that dice rolling is easy at the casino through the first roll, when it is your turn around the table and the dice are pushed to you on the big table. One must remember that if you roll a number 2 on the dice or a number 3 or 12 showing a total on the dice, you lose, and the dice goes to the next person at the table. You lose or win the money you put on the table in front of you.

You can wait until it is your turn to throw the dice or you can bet on anyone's roll as they start. The point number which is or can be made on your first roll is 4-5-6-8-9-or 10. If you roll your point first before you roll a 7 you win.

"I get it now—sort of," Ruthie said. "Doesn't the casino have an edge in this normally?"

"Yes," he retorted, "It is how one throws the dice to the other end of the table—it seems like I found a holy area. Even though the house still has an advantage, because the easiest number to roll is a seven.

They went the very next weekend to the

casino. Monte also promised Ruthie a dinner. When they got to the crap table, she stood a little back of him as it was quite soon when it became his turn to throw the dice. There were about eight people betting around the table so it did not take long. Monte put $25 dollars down and rolled a 7. Of course the number seven is the easiest number to come up.

That is why the casino has an edge, he explained to Ruthie between rolls of the dice. Monte then rolled a 7 eight more times to get off to an unusually good start. Throwing a 7 on the first roll, or an 11, is a winner. Then he made five separate points in a row.

"Not easy to make the point," Ruthie said, as she remembered how he had explained that part of the game to her.

The patrons around the table became louder, kept cheering and yelling through the entire time Monte had the dice. He held them for more than 20 minutes. Patrons who were playing at the slot machines or blackjack heard the noise from the crap table area and came over. The crowd became huge watching the action as it continued to take place.

Monte and Ruthie left the table right after he

finally sevened out. The applause and congrats were still ringing in his ear. Monte noticed that one of the   pit bosses (who was working among the crap tables to watch the casino employees, as the game moved around the players), was looking right at Monte and Ruthie in a peculiar way.

The man edged out from behind the tables and approached Monte. "Nice rollin' son," he said in a pleasant tone.

Monte said, "Thanks." The man asked him if he was from around the area, and offered to buy him and his friend dinner at the hotel's dining room.

Monte was surprised, but declined the offer. He and Ruthie took the bus trip back to their homes and did not give it any more thought. They went to a local restaurant.

Then Monte walked Ruthie home and went in and sat with her on the couch. He told her a little more about the 'pit men' and their duties amongst the   multiple crap tables.

The door opened a few minutes later, and Ruthie's father, Ralph, came in the door and saw them sitting close together, (which was all right as they were   getting a little bit more serious with each other). He had been told by Ruthie of the earlier success Monte was having, so he said to him "Did you have any success this time at the casino again today?"

Monte said, "Yes, I've been very lucky. I don't know if it will continue." Ruthie's father then asked his daughter if she had a good time and she said, "It was more interesting once I saw and understood how the game is played with all the rules involved."

Ruthie's father said he knew some of the rules, but never played it. But he explained to them he had a friend from his high-school days who was now a top executive at the casino where Monte was having success. So he had called this friend (who had heard of Monte) and invited him for dinner tomorrow night right there. Perhaps he could tell them all about those items that are important and which the public has little knowledge of.

Monte did go over the next night for dinner, and the man entered the house a few minutes later, along with his son who looked about 30 years of age. The son's name was Elmore. The son kept staring steadily at Monte. His father was a much more pleasant person. He said to

Monte, "I heard you did very well playing craps. I did not see it, but certainly heard about it."

Before Monte could respond to the man, his son, Elmore, rudely interrupted and loudly said "Would you just tell us how you did it?" Monte noticed the mean look on his face, contorted and with an angrier look than he had ever seen on anyone.

Monte replied, "I just rolled the dice and the numbers I needed kept coming up on the dice."

Elmore's father interjected quickly, "Be nice, Elmore, talk nice."

Elmore looked quickly at his father, then turned back to Monte and in a gruff manner said he never had heard of anyone ever throwing dice from one end of the table to the other and rolling eight 7s in a row.

Elmore's father was uncomfortable and annoyed with his son's tone of voice, so he stood up and stated strongly, "We are going to leave now!"

Once they had gone, Rachel's father stated that he was surprised that his friend had brought his son, Elmore, along. Conversation had not gone as he had planned. As far as he could remember, Elmore had only recently got out of prison after a conviction of assault for two separate attacks on elderly women.

Monte took Ruthie with him on each of his next five trips to the casino, betting a little more with each successful happening on each visit. He did take Ruthie to the casino restaurant every time. He was trying to not let it go to his head, this odd way of playing craps, and was realizing it was still luck that was occurring.

It was just the number of times that it won that disturbed him. On the way out after their latest visit, he thought he saw Elmore peeking out from behind one of the pillars near the exit area.

They both got on the bus and Ruthie got off a block from her house as usual, but noticed a car stopped behind the bus and in the car was Elmore. She was stunned. She ran as fast as she could to her house. She barged through the door and yelled for her father. He was reading the newspaper. She was almost out of breath yet told her father, "Elmore was following the bus I and Monte were on. Please do something, Dad! I am scared!" Ruthie's father got up and went to the phone.

Meanwhile Monte got off the bus a few yards from his house and noticed that lights were on at Alex's house across the street and thought he would go over later and tell Alex of his recent success.

Monte walked into his house; turned the lights on and went towards the TV so he could watch some of it and relaxed first. He heard the door open and he thought it was Alex, but, no, it was Elmore, and he was shocked. Monte was very frightened and did not know how Elmore had found his home. Better be nice, he thought.

Elmore just gave him a dirty look. "Are you switching the dice? If you're that lucky I can't believe it."

Monte replied, "I just throw the dice. I just have been very lucky."

As Elmore walked toward him, he reached in his back pocket and took out a long knife. Putting it sharply on Monte's left arm Elmore said "Where's the money?"

Monty was really scared. He said "I don't have it here. I put it in the bank."

Elmore said, "No you haven't. I saw you walk in here right from the casino." Just then the door opened and in rushed Alex. He walked straight up to Elmore, and pushed him harshly away from Monte and onto the floor. Elmore still had the knife in his hand but he soon realized he was over matched and out-witted by this bigger man.

The door opened again, and there was Ruthie's father. He took one look at the situation. Then he walked quickly over to Elmore, took the knife away, grabbed his arm, and pulled him up off the floor. He held him close to him, however. And to the room, he said, "Ruthie came into the house after getting off the bus and was upset because she had seen Elmore in his car, following the bus from behind."

Ruthie's father said he had immediately called Alex, explained the situation, and urged him to go over to Monte's house right away. And then he went out and started his car.

Table Talk
Virginia Braxton

"What the fuck!" I thought as the discrete, dark limo pulled up at a gated entrance labelled "Lily Valley Elite Independent Living."

The feds had promised they would keep me alive and hide me well, while I was waiting to testify at the big trial. They'd given me the alias of "Tom Carpenter," and some info about his/my fictitious life—He was a dull guy, single, and worked for years at an Amazon shipping center. I should be able to handle that. In my earlier days I had acted and and done improved. Guess I'll have to revive those skills in order to keep my anonymity.

But, still, I didn't expect an old folks home!

I'm only 39, but, truthfully, my life expectancy is probably shorter than that of most the folks here.

My handlers had arranged for me to be lodged in one of the private cottages. They'd installed extra   electronics around my building, and a huge TV in my living room.

They waited while I unpacked, handed me my Lily Valley Resident nametag to wear, and pointed me   toward the dining room. They thought I should at least make an appearance.

Since we were still under partial Covid restrictions, I masked up, and then put on the all-encompassing dark glasses I'd picked up somewhere. Maybe I should get some of those mirrored aviator glasses that Tonton Macoute used to wear. People get so busy looking at their own reflection that they don't notice the face around the glasses.

Anyway, I thought it would help me fit in if I seemed uncertain on my feet—I'd been proud of being fit—so I shuffled my way to the dining room.

I asked an attendant where I should sit, and she pointed me to a table with three women. I asked permission to join them, and they gestured to the empty seat.

The one with the died brown hair said, "I haven't seen you before. You must be new here. I'm Gladia, and you are ...?"

"Tom," I said, trying to read my nametag upside down. "Yes, I just moved in this afternoon."

Gladia introduced Molly and Bethany, our two table companions.

Molly smiled at me, and said, "What brought you to Lily Valley Elite? Do you have family in the area?"

Before I could respond, Gladia said, "Yes, I saw those three young men helping you move in. Are they relatives? Is that why you're here?"

"Yes," I said, "They wanted me where they could look after me." A rare true statement for me, I thought.

Gladia went on, "I think it's so nice when family members look after each other. Are they your sons?"

"Nephews," I improvised, well aware that my newly acquired "nephews" were older than me.

"Do they live in the area, so you have someone outside the community who is keeping track of you?"

"Yes, they're good at that, even though we have different lifestyles."

"So, do their parents live in this area?"

"No. Rosie died."

Molly broke in, "You seem a little young to be a resident here. Is there any special reason?"

"Well," I paused while thinking frantically, "The doctors at Stanford are working on my case—they say it's 'interesting,' but they haven't come up with anything yet. Hope you're never an 'interesting' case. The doctors get all excited, but they don't help much.

"Look," I said, pushing back my chair. "I hope you'll excuse me, but the move and its confusion has really tired me out, and I think I'd better lie down now." I barely remembered to shuffle on my way back to the apartment.

Agent Bronkowski was on alert when I put my key in the lock, but relaxed when I came in alone.

"Well, Bronk," I said, "Meet your Uncle Tom."

"Who?"

"Me. And Agents Johnson and Lowell are also my nephews."

"But Johnson is pure sub-Saharan African."

"Well, blame Rosie."

"Who's Rosie?"

"Your mother."

"Oh. Where did all of this come from?" Bronk asked, shaking his head and frowning.

"The women I sat with at dinner. They think they're being friendly, and they kept pressing me for details about my family. Talk about interrogation! So I made up stuff, and now we all have to remember it.

"Incidentally, I also have some kind of rare disease."

"What disease is that?" queried Bronk, who knew that I'd been given a thorough physical before I was brought here.

"I told them that the doctors at Stanford haven't been able to decide what it is, but they're studying me closely. That way, I can avoid specifics, but I have an excuse to get away from the women, or this place, for that matter."

Just then Bronk got the signal that Johnson was arriving, and a few minutes later opened the door to him.

"How's it going?" he asked.

"Well," said Bronk, "You and I are now Tom's nephews. We're half-brothers. Our mother was Rosie, who is dead. Tom has a mysterious disease which the doctors at Stanford are struggling to identify. He's an 'interesting case.'"

"Do we have a story for why I spend the night here?"

I broke in, "Oh, your wife kicked you out, so you're crashing on my sofa."

"So I took refuge with you when Rosie—"

"No," I said, "Rosie's your mother. She's dead. Pick a name for your wife."

I told the handlers that I needed more channels. I also decided it would add atmosphere if I had a cane, so I asked the handlers to get me one. "Maybe you could find a sword-cane," I said wistfully, but what they produced was only an ordinary metal cane with a four-prong base.

Johnson sighed. "I'm Tom's nephew by his deceased sister, Rosie, and I'm here because my wife, Stella kicked me out."

There was a knock on the door. I peered through the spyhole. It was a tiny, frail looking woman. I nodded to Bronc and Johnson, and they went in the bedroom, before I opened the door a little way.

"Hello, Tom Carpenter," she chirped. "I'm Clarisse, your building ambassador, and I'm here to welcome you to Lily Valley. Here," she said, handing me a bag, "are a few things you might need as you settle in.

"Is there anything I can do for you? I know you have those nephews who are keeping a real close eye on you, but there may be some things about Lily Valley itself that I can help you with. And remember, if you ever need help, just push the button on your alarm, and someone will come. I'll stop by this evening so you can go to the dining room with me and meet some more of us."

"Thank, you," I said, taking the bag from her, "I'll probably stay in this evening. I feel a headache coming."

"Oh, in that case you can order dinner and eat in your room. Just call the front desk. Do you have the number? And then leave your dishes outside your door."

"That's good to know," I said desperately, "but tonight my nephew (which one? I thought) is planning to cook for me. Now, if you'll excuse me, I really must go."

"Of course," said Clarisse. "Well, goodbye for now." As she turned to leave, I smiled at her before shutting the door and heaving a sigh of relief.

"Nice, friendly place here," commented Johnson. "A real community. They share the news."

The next morning I masked up and went to the dining room for breakfast. I saw an empty seat at a table with three men sitting at it and approached them.

"Mind if I join you?" I asked.

"Of course, not," said one. "I'm Lou, and these are Steve and George. We're always glad to have another male here at Lily Valley. The gals outnumber us, about three to one, but I hear that's a very good ratio compared with other senior facilities."

"Thank you, Lou," I said seating myself. "What's on the breakfast menu?"

Lou and Steve started to speak at the same time, but Steve won out. "I hear you go up to the Stanford Medical Center regularly. So do I. Maybe we could share rides some time, and do our part to spare the air?"

'Well," I said, "I don't think my doctor would want me in close continuous contact with someone who's outside my 'pod.'"

"Don't tell me you're contagious! I'm surprised they let you in Lilly Valley!"

"Not contagious. No, my immune system is very weak, but as far as I know, I'm not contagious. The doctors don't think I should accept rides from anybody but my nephews.

Well, here's our wait person," I said, glad for the diversion.

"I'd like two eggs easy over and a pancake. Also berries. I already have my coffee." For the rest of the meal I avoided answering questions by pointing to my full mouth.

I shuffled back to my apartment to find that Agent Lowell had arrived. He politely inquired if anything had happened since he'd last seen me.

I responded, "Well, I have a mysterious disease that the Stanford doctors have not been able to identify. It greatly weakens my immune system, but is not contagious. They don't want me in close or continuous contact with anyone but my nephews."

"Who are they?"

"You, Bronk and Johnson."

"Yeah," sighed Johnson. "He's told people that we all are his nephews by his deceased sister Rosie, and my wife is Stella."

"But what about Peggy?" queried Lowell, who knew and liked Johnson's wife, Peggy.

"Stella's my fictional wife," said Johnson a bit huffily. "This has nothing to do with Peggy."

I decided to have a headache for the rest of the day, and stayed in my room.

We decided that one meal a day in the dining room would be my limit, so I didn't venture out until noon the next day.

I masked up and, leaning on my new cane, shuffled my way to the dining room. There was an empty seat at a table with people I had not met so far, so I joined them. They shared names, and when I said I was Tom Carpenter, one of the women said, "Oh! You must be the man with all the nephews!"

"Yes," I answered.

"Maybe I shouldn't say this, but they don't look at all alike—not like a family."

"No," I said repressively, "The family doesn't talk about that. And you are ...?"

"Stephanie," she replied, but just all me 'Steph.'"

Another woman broke in, "I'm envious of all the time your nephews spend with you. How do they do it?"

"Well, they're in business for themselves, so their time is at their discretion."

"Tech entrepreneurs?"

"No, they're junk dealers. They sort through the stuff that people throw out. They make some interesting finds, worth good money, but they can control when they work."

"But—"

"To tell the truth," I said mendaciously, "They're really looking for Grandpa's, (well, their great grandfather's) gold. The family legend is that he was a highway robber, who never was caught, and he hid a pile of gold somewhere."

"Ohhh," one of the others said, "You should talk to Grant, over there. His hobby is old time highway robbers, and he has lots of pictures. You might even find a family resemblance!

"Oh, dear, Grant just left, but I'll tell him about you and introduce you at dinner."

"Well, Grandpa wasn't widely known, because he never got caught. Now, if you'll excuse me, it's time for me to rest," I said, and fled to my apartment.

I hadn't been there very long when Agent Lowell came on duty. As he set down a medium size case and a bundle, he inquired, "What's the news today?"

"Well," I said, You three are junk dealers, making good money, but what you're really looking for is Grandpa's, (I mean your great-grandfather's,) gold. He was a highway robber who was never caught and Grant wants to show me pictures of highway robbers to see if there is a family resemblance."

Lowell gave a faint moan. "This has gone on long enough.

"Johnson," he said, "you stay a bit longer, while I go make some calls from the secure phone in the car."

When he returned, he said briskly, "Carpenter, you have 45 minutes to pack up. We're sending you to an isolated mountain top, a place with no neighbors for you to chat with."

The discrete black limo pulled up outside my building. As agent Lowell handed me in, he gave me the case and bundle he had brought with him that day.

"Here, he said, "it's an old portable typewriter doesn't need electricity and I put in a new ribbon. And here's some paper. You can make up all the stories you like while you're sitting on that mountain top waiting for the trial," and the limo pulled away with me in it.

The Bones of a Mammoth
By Virginia Braxton

Maria pulled the car into her driveway, turned off the ignition, and sighed. She realized she was avoiding going into the house, because she dreaded dealing with her 14 year old nephew, Tom.

Although given the opportunity to go with his parents, Tom was staying with her while they were gone for the summer on an expedition studying plant life in the Arctic Tundra. At the last moment, to his parents' consternation, Tom had refused to go with them, declaring plants "Boooring!" He carried on so, that his parents relented, and Maria offered to have him stay with her, in what Tom termed "civilization."

Now Maria wished she hadn't made the offer. She had hoped Tom would provide a little companionship as she rattled around in the house, which seemed to have doubled in size since her husband's death, but Tom had immersed himself in some secret project, taking over the spare room, filling it with all kinds of electronic equipment, and barely speaking to her. Maria wondered if he were trying to build a time machine.

Inside, she collected Tom for his weekly Zoom meeting with his parents, Zach and Sue, and sat down to watch. Her sister, Sue, was unusually animated.

"The most exciting thing has happened," Sue said. "Usually the biggest drawback to the expedition is the isolation, being with the same handful of people twenty-four seven, but this year there are two, two I said, other expeditions in this area. So we've combined into one central camp just a mile or two from each of our sites."

Tom asked, "Are all of you studying dead plants?"

"Oh no," Sue replied. "One expedition is from NOAA—"

"Noah," interrupted Tom, "Who cares about that old legend, and besides, I thought the ark was stuck on Mt. Ararat!"

"NOAA," said Zach authoritatively, "is the National Oceanographic Atmospheric Administration which is part of the U.S. government and operates out of D.C. It's responsible for the weather satellites, among other things. This expedition is studying the release of methane gas, by the permafrost as it melts." Tom made a gagging noise.

"What about the other expedition?" asked Maria.

"Well, they are from the University of Montana and they are excavating a cache of mammoth bones—"Mammoth bones! Mom, Dad, can I come? Maybe I could help them!" burst out Tom.

The adults were speechless.

"See," continued Tom, "That's what I've been   trying to do. Bring a mammoth back to life!"

"In my house?" cried Maria.

"Well, only the head, but I need more space,"   continued Tom. "And I could learn so much more if I could see some actual bones!"

"Hmmmmm," said Zach, exchanging looks with Sue. "How do we know you wouldn't change your mind again, when you couldn't watch movies on the Internet, or as soon as you encountered the mosquitoes, which are about the size of chipmunks?"

"Scout's honor," said Tom.

"You quit scouts last year because you said they only did stupid things."

"You mean my promise wouldn't count? Please let me come!"

"Tom, expeditions are serious business. They have to be planned, and money found to support them—that's no small item—and the competition to go on one is very stiff. Not very many people get to go."

"But you were going to take me. I got my passport and all my gear is over at the house. I won't mess up. I'll be really careful."

Zach paused and then said: "Tom, raise your right hand and repeat after me" and Tom did.

"I, Thomas Grantly Brown, swear on the bones of a mammoth,
To abide by the rules of all three expeditions,
To never remove my geolocater,
To cheerfully do what is asked of me,
And to protect the work of the expeditions,
On my honor as a scientist."

Then Zach put out his hand and mimed a handshake with Tom.

Sue wiped tears from her eyes and said, "But how are you going to get here? You're only 14, you've never travelled by yourself, and you only speak one language!"

"Aunt Maria, could you take me? You only have the Garden Club to keep you here."

"Well," replied Maria, "I still have a valid passport from the trip Ben and I were planning to take when he died. I'd just have to get a visa."

"And bring your cameras," said Sue, "the scenery here is phenomenal."

Five days later, Maria and Tom boarded a northbound plane. Tom had been angelic, but Maria was exhausted and fell asleep as soon as the plane was airborne. She was woken by the announcement that they were approaching the airport and would everyone prepare for landing.

As soon as they were through with the formalities, they spotted Zach and another man outside the barrier, and hurried to them.

As Tom hugged Zach, he asked, "Where's Mom?"

"Plane's too small," replied Zach. "Maria, meet Ed, our bush pilot. Ed, meet my sister-in-law, Maria, and my son, Tom."

"Glad to meet you," said Ed. "Let's get moving. There's someone at the campsite who's very anxious to see you, Tom," and he led the way across the   tarmac to his plane. Before they started, Zach gave them their geo-locators. Then, to Tom's delight, he was permitted to sit in the co-pilot's seat, after promising not to touch anything.

At the campsite, the members of all three expeditions were assembled for dinner. Ed stopped with them to eat, and then, as he was climbing back into his plane, he turned to Maria and said, "I'll pick you up in five days, when I bring in the next load of supplies."

Maria did her best to meet all the members of all three expeditions and to remember all their names, but Tom immediately attached himself to a tall lean man who was introduced as the leader of the group digging for mammoths bones.

"Tom," the man said, "I'm Sven Torngren with the expedition focused on the mammoth bones. Your dad has told me of your interest in them. Would you like to come along tomorrow and watch us work?"

Tom accepted enthusiastically, and the next morning happily rolled out of his sleeping bag. When they returned to camp in the evening, he ate dinner, and promptly went to bed without Zach having a chance to talk with him.

When the same thing happened the next day, Zach and Sue found Sven and asked him how Tom was doing.

"He's really great," replied Sven. "I wish all the graduate students were as meticulous as he is!" (His parents blinked at this description of Tom.) "And he's cheerful, too. Of course, he doesn't yet have the academic background that the others have, but he's just soaking up information, asking questions, and trying to put it all together. Today, I saw him making some notes, and he showed me a reading list he's compiling for himself. Most of the books are textbooks I use in my classes that he'd heard about from the grad students."

"Well, I guess he's found his vocation," said Zach. "We were worried about him, but you seemed to have worked a miracle with him."

"It wasn't me," said Sven, "it was the mammoths. And even if he eventually gives up mammoths, he's learning how to gather evidence and reason from it in a disciplined way. That's good training for any scientist, or for that matter, for life in general."

Maria had gone with Tom the first morning and photographed the mammoth bones, but having no   assigned role in the camp, she was restless. Then Jim, one of the NOAA scientists, said to her over dinner, "I notice you have some fine cameras with you.   Methanes's not particularly photographic, but there are some things which might appeal to your eye on the walk to our work site. Would you like to come with me tomorrow morning?"

"That would be fun," she said. For the next three days, she followed Jim around, taking pictures and chatting with him, when it did not interfere with his work. Nonetheless, she was eagerly waiting when Ed returned with his plane. She wanted to get home and start playing with her photos.

As she was leaving, Jim said, "I hope we can get together when we're back in the lower 40. I'd really like to see what you do with those images."

"I'd like that too," she said.

"Dad," said Tom to Zach, one evening, "You know that application you got for me to attend the STEM school? It's still on my desk at home, because I thought I didn't want to go there, but now I do. And the deadline's in three days. Is there any way we can fill it out from here?"

Zach took a deep breath, stifled several retorts, and asked, "What would your focus be?"

"Well" said Tom, "Sven says that I should start with earth sciences as soon as possible before I specialize in mammoths. I don't think they teach paleoecology there, but I could take whatever is closest to it. In the meantime, I would study statistics which he says is fundamental to any scientific work these days. And they have an alternate language option, where you don't have to take Spanish or German as a foreign language. You can take, like, the language your grandparents speak, or something else. I think some of the kids are taking Mandarin and others Arabic. I'd take either Russian or Norwegian."

After 36 hours of struggle with a fitful Internet connection, Tom's application had been submitted and Zach was catching up on his sleep, when Tom burst into the tent, exclaiming, "Dad! Dad! Look what Sven gave me!" and holding out a brown rock.

Zach looked at the rock. He could not see why Tom was so excited. "What is it?"

"It's fossilized mammoth poop! Sven gave it to me so I can study it. Tomorrow, we're going to slice it open. And look at these papers. They say it was removed legally for scientific study, and I own it. You'd better keep the papers safe in case we have trouble with customs. Sven says we must have found a poop dump, because there's so much there I can have one."

"Put the papers in the green satchel with our passports, and it's 'dung' not 'poop.' I'll look at it in the morning. Now go away and let me sleep."

The next morning both Sue and Zach attended the ceremonial slicing of the dung. Sue put the slice under her microscope and invited Tom to take the first look.

"Gosh, Mom, did you mix up the slides? It looks just like the plants you look at all the time."

Sue took a look. "You're right. I don't understand how it could go through the mammoth's digestive system intact. It's an interesting anomaly. I didn't realize that my plants were that old, but there's no doubt about them being in the mammoth dung. We'll have to get more specimens."

"That's easy," said Tom, "There's plenty of po—dung there. I'll collect more for you, if it's okay with Sven."

From then on Tom spent the mornings collecting samples of fossilized mammoth dung, which were then sliced. He examined them in the afternoon on his mother's microscope while she annotated and catalogued her own findings.

Night had started again and was rapidly lengthening, when they all broke camp and were air lifted to the airport. There they found uncommon congestion. Due to a terrible storm south of them, all flights were cancelled. The airport officials informed them that although the year-round residents of the tiny town had opened their homes to stranded travelers, they were full up, and the scientists would have to camp out in the airport. The officials reassured them that they had plenty of food available and emergency power.

"I guess we cut it too close," said Jim from NOAA, "and I knew it was going to be dicey. Oh well, it could be worse."

"But I'll be late for school opening," wailed Tom, who had been accepted at the STEM school and was looking forward to it.

"Stuff happens," said Jim. "You have to roll with it. We'd better unpack our sleeping bags."

Thirty-six hours later, they finally boarded a southbound plane to Dulles airport near Washington D.C. They were greeted by Maria, who visited with Jim while they were sorting out their luggage.

Tom, who had slept through most of the flight, was in a frenzy to get home. "I have to be at school for orientation in six hours," he kept reminding everyone.

Maria responded calmly, "The rush hour traffic hasn't started yet, so we should be at your house in half an hour. That will give you enough time clean up. Your mom told me that you'd had a growth spurt and needed to go shopping, but you won't have to go to school with your ankles hanging out, because I let down the cuffs on those pants you didn't like." At the house, she pointed Tom in the direction of the shower, and Sue and Zach toward the kitchen, where Zach immediately made coffee.

When Tom made his well-scrubbed reappearance, the adults saw a slim youth, with long hair wearing pants that covered him decently, but no shirt. "My shirts are too tight," he explained.

"Well," said Maria, I made something for you," and handed him a gift-wrapped package. He opened it and found a sweatshirt, and on the front and back were beautiful Arctic scenes of the place they had just left. Dominating each scene were photos of mammoth bones.

"Oh, oh! Auntie! Now people will ask me what these are and I can tell them all about my mammoths," crowed Tom crushing her in a hug.

"Now hurry up and get in the car, or we'll be late for school," said Maria with a pleased smile.

Zach looked after the departing car and remarked, "And she hasn't even seen the slides of the mammoth dung yet."

"Bet she will have by the time he goes to bed," responded Sue.

Zach groaned, "I think we've created a monster."

"No," quipped Sue, "only a mammoth. I, for one, am going to go soak in a leisurely bubble bath."

"Now that sounds enticing," responded Zach with a smile.

Artificial Vida
By Kent Humpal

Janene pulled her car into the visitors parking space. Wow, parking was really limited for such a large community, she thought. Leaving her car, she placed a Press Pass on the dash and looked at the building's surrounding landscaping and rather stark entryway. The plantings were evergreen, low-water shrubs, pretty drab.

She moved back, held up her phone and took several photos of the the grounds were so ordinary she ignored them. This is not only spare, but ugly, she thought. Moving to the doorway, she noticed she had to buzz to get inside. A young woman appeared, wearing a floral pink and green short jacket over a subdued work uniform. On the pocket was "Casa Vida Dulce" in bright yellow.

"Yes, can I help you?" asked a soft voice.

"I'm Janene Fuller, from the regional newspaper. I have an appointment with the manager, Mr. Trent, I believe. We have an interview arranged. I hope he's not tied up—the traffic was horrible."

"Just wait here and I'll call him. There is our coffee—our soft drink machine's over by the elevator if you need anything. I'm sorry—it only takes cash."

Janene looked over the entry/lounge area as she strolled over to the pseudo-oil and watercolor paintings. Colorful, but not very exciting she thought, again taking a few shots with her phone before anyone came for her.

"I'm sorry, I should have introduced myself," pointing at her plastic badge, "my name is Erica. I oversee entry and exit, deliveries, and any visitors for our clients."

As she turned to her left, she introduced the man coming from a small, private elevator. "This is Mr. Scanlon, our manager. He is also our Business Officer. Mr. Scanlon, Ms. Fuller is from the local newspaper, but you already know that from your calendar, I'm sure."

"Uh yes, nice to meet you, Ms. Fuller. How can I help you?"

He was early middle aged and polished in appearance. As Janene extended her hand, she took a more careful inspection. The hand she shook was soft, the nails manicured but not polished. The clothes were better than most middle management but the shoes and tie were upper class. No glasses, but no squint either. Probably laser surgery. His smile was gleaming. "I bet those are good caps," she thought, "better than mine."

"Well, several of us at the *Valley Fog* are intrigued by your advertisements and endorsements. Especially the endorsements — they all seem to be from family members, such as children, legal guardians, but seldom from an actual patron. Also, a few of our staff are of retirement age and older. They're beginning to look at age fifty-five or older housing and down sizing from their present homes. Several would like to pass their homes on to family, but would have to sell them to afford most places. Your facility, 'Casa Vida Dulce' is the only one that meets the low cost criteria. They wonder how you can do it.

"I'm here not only as a social reporter but to gather information for my readers and also for my friends at *The Fog*. You do know our slogan, 'not to obfuscate, but to educate?' That's what I hope to do."

"Well, Ms. Fuller, may I call you Janene? Just call me Lyle. We're just a big family, here, you see, very informal. We are the first of what our founders hope will be a series of group virtual life living facilities. Eventually apartments, hotels, even prisons may be set up in this way."

Just then a small group of occupants came through a side door from what seemed to be a lounge. A quick glimpse gave the impression of cheap Scandia tables and chairs, and a litter of paper cups, off-brand candy bars, and chips. Janene heard jumbled conversations as the people moved toward a large elevator.

"I didn't know elephants were so tall, and they swayed as they walked."

"The camels did too, remarked another guest." They were turning off and removing glasses and headgear with large goggle-like eye pieces and either head-phones or ear-buds as they disappeared.

"A Grizzly Bear almost smacked me with a salmon," leaked out of the elevator as doors closed.

"What was that?" Janene asked as the lights indicating the floors flashed rapidly upward.

"As I was just about to explain, ours is a virtual living experience. Everyone moving in gets Virtual Experiencing equipment to suit their needs, or financial circumstances of their physical or uh, financial situation."

"Do you mean everything the clients experience or feel is via virtual means, simulating equipment?" asked Janene.

"Well, a great deal of it, possibly all in some circumstances. I'm not sure—it's all transmitted back to the main office. They like to compare data from the various facilities."

"Let me get this correct: Almost everything is on a Virtual Reality program. Does that mean that the various travel, entertainment venues such as concerts, plays, and musicals, are on VR sources?"

"Oh, certainly. Our patrons can sit in their own apartments, our center, anywhere on the grounds and receive the programming and feel like they're right in the best seats of the theatre. It's marvelous, and they only pay a basic fee each month regardless of how much, how many times, they use it."

"What about trips? I heard the group entering the elevator discussing out of the area trips."

"Well, we do have emergency alternatives, but we have no busses. We have VR trips to every national park in the world, scenic areas, safaris, archaeology digs, museums, and even battlefield experiences for those interested. No bus, no driver, no liability, means no insurance.

We encourage Zoom medical visits and have contracted with Gofer Car service. Clients get a 20 per cent discount," explained Lyle. "Our programmed robot visits each room and dispenses meds, makes sure the clients take them."

Janene looked at him quizzically and asked another question. "What about the grounds? You're basically a five story high-rise plus basement. There seems to be little on the grounds that supports the pictures in your advertisements and pamphlets of beautiful shrubs, trees, or flowers."

"Well, if you would let me loan you the VR gear, we have some for some family members looking to place relatives."

As Janene placed the VR glasses and headphones on, Lyle pushed a switch. "You can adjust for clarity and brightness with the little knob. The button above the right brow activates the little fans and odor dispensers. No allergies from our gardens." Janene's senses were flooded with the colors of bright blooming plants against various shades of green. After a minute of virtual stroll, she shut it down.

"Well, that was certainly an experience, almost as good as reality."

"We think so," Lyle replied. "We even have hikes from the Grand Canyon to New Zealand, even sports activities, like fishing and golf."

"What are your food services like? What's available? Is there a dining area or do most people eat in their rooms?"

"Well, there are still some clients that like social contact, but even at mealtimes we encourage the use of VR equipment. We can get by with grade A meats and less expensive vegetables and fruits. Now advise your readers, it is not less nutritious, but a little less photogenic, maybe chewier. But if you're wearing the VR gear and activating the blowers, everything looks better and smells delicious. The desserts are especially scrumptious," said Lyle.

Just then the elevator doors opened and dislodged a group of patrons. Most carrying their VR gear, a few without.

"I can hardly wait for the weekend. Even if it's nasty, it will be real. I know my grandson is playing in a ball game, real time dust and stink."

"My granddaughters have a recital. It will be fun errors and all," the voices came out of the elderly crowd.

"I hope you got enough information—we can use all the good reviews. Corporate keeps a close watch over any news or critical reports," said Lyle, anxiously as he pressed a buzzer to let Janene exit.

Janene muttered to herself as she walked to her car. "What a horrible way to live! Hardly anything was real—I couldn't live this way!"

Retrieving her phone from her bag, she pressed the app that opened the door, pressed another that started the engine, and as she climbed in, moved the seat forward and adjusted it. Janene spoke to the dash board screen.

"Siri, activate the climate control and bring up the map for my next stop. Oh, and show me any calls that came in while I was out."

The safety and warning apps checked in. She pressed the button for self-driving as she plugged in her laptop at the consul port.

"Boy that was a terrible glimpse of the future, like 1984. I couldn't stand it," she muttered as her seat adjusted, the locks clicked, and the car guided itself out of the lot.

Full Circle
By Kent Humpal

The room was brightly lit after several days of subdued and somber light. As his eyes became accustomed to his situation, he became aware of the surroundings. "Where am I?" he asked the masked faces that entered his vision.

"Saints Joseph and Mary Hospital, Mr. Larson," came a soft voice, obviously female, from the nearest mask. They were all wearing soft blue or green scrubs, and it was hard to tell them apart, even their gender, from his position.

"How long have I been here," he asked huskily, "and why?"

Another hand and face entered his view, with a plastic cup of water and a straw. "Here, take a sip, sir, we only removed the tube a while ago."

The liquid soothed his throat and he looked around. Because of the wall mirror, he could see the whole room. Unusual, he thought, they generally let only two or three family members in at a time, but the room is full. There's Martha, her eyes red and puffy. Oh, there're my son and daughter. He called out to them, "Hey, Jeff, Jilly, where are the kids?" but apparently they couldn't hear him.

They all crowded around: wife, kids, in-laws, and even the grandkids reached for him, touching, caressing him, speaking softly. "How do you feel, Dad? You look better. Can you remember anything?

"The doctors said you had a heart seizure, but the car wreck was the main issue," said Curt, his eldest.

"Try to limit your talk. He is in very critical condition. It's touch and go yet," said a calm voice from the side. "He is very weak, you can see from the monitors his instability."

"I love you all, remember that," he barely whispered, as he closed his eyes.

They looked on sadly, as the lights on the monitor began to flicker and slowly shut down. The doctors and nurses worked frantically to regain control, but nothing worked.

The family looked at his calm, smiling face. As life flickered out, Paul Larson was unaware of the monitor's flickering lights. He was absorbed by the great, bright light that seemed to absorb him and transport him upward and away.

Ranulf and the Dragon
By Kent Humpal

Ranulf roused himself and hailed the watchman at the town gate. It was dusk and his small retinue straggled over the bridged moat, through the narrow passage, and emerged into the small village square. The group was comprised of himself, his squire, Cerdic, and the groom/page Ordo. A small cart followed pulled by an equally small pony. Walking alongside was an equally small man, a merchant of sundries, cloth, needles, thread, wooden thimbles, occasionally a holy relic authenticated by the bishop of a nearby Abbey. His wife traveled with him, a young woman, stout of build and temper.

Ranulf and his men had been out a fortnight following rumors and complaints—pleas for relief relayed to Lord Morantz from his holdings. The last three days had been spent almost entirely on horseback, except at the inn, where the merchant had set up a stall. He granted the man, Wilferd of Stouten, safe passage for a packet of needles, a small bauble, and a doll for his little daughter, Yaraine. His wife, Ursula, was of Saxon descent but liked the sound and pretentions of the Welsh-Cornish name. He called her Iggie when he told her sleep stories.

"Cerdics," he called out, "Take Roland and the other horses to the stables. Make sure the boys rub them down and feed them grain. It's been a long trip for them as well. Ordo, if you please, rack the saddles and gear, and stow the baggage. You can do the cleaning and oiling, whatever you think needs to be repaired or replaced, tomorrow."

As he entered the rooms allotted to him, three rooms and a small alcove for his daughter, he shrugged off his cloak and felt warmth coming off the wall shared with the castle ovens. A favored location for a long-time retainer and childhood playmate of Lord Morantz, holder of the castle and fief of the local Baron. Ursula came in from the bed chamber, "Ronny, get that ratty, smelly, tunic and armor out of here. You make the mitten smell sweet."

"A fine greeting for a tired, worn knight, milady," said Ranulf as he dutifully undid the buckles, slid off the curse, dumped the clothing and gathered her up in a hearty, lusty embrace.

Near naked, he kissed her while she struggled briefly, then gave into his kisses. His ardor sank silently as Yaraine came running and hugged her father's legs.

"Daddy, daddy did you bring me anything, did you slay me a dragon?"

"Well, wait 'til Cerdics comes round tomorrow. There may be something in our packs," smiled Ronny as he picked up his daughter. "I didn't go into any big towns, or villages this trip."

The armorer looked over the helmet, breast plate, and chain hauberk checking for dents, gouges, and damaged hinges. Draping the chain mail over a stand, he looked for rents and worn links. "Well, no scorches or melted spots, no dragons with flaming breath. That's good."

They were both aware that dragons flying or otherwise, were no longer around, if they ever existed. Only occasional skull or partial skeleton unearthed in the quarries or uncovered by floods kept the legends alive.

"I'll have it ready for you by the next trip. My apprentices will have it tumbled, oil the joints and hinges by next week. By the way,

Morantz wants you to report by noon. He said to come to his book room. You can give me the true story at the tavern tonight."

Cerdics and Ordo met Ranulf at the entrance to his chamber.

"Roland was greeted warmly by the mare, Ranulf. He didn't appear to be worn down." Cerdics greeted Ranulf with a smile.

Ordo spoke up, "The packages are on the table near the fireplace." As Ursula entered, she asked about Ordo's wife and Cerdics betrothed. Pleased at the attention, they ducked their heads and grinned.

Ordo spoke again, "My wife wonders if you could help her with the new gown for Lady Matilda. She would like to have it when the Baron and his cortege show up, (you know the competition between Marantz's Lady and the Baroness). You know they always come about the time of harvest and new ale. They eat and drink and move on."

Ranulf spoke softly to Ursula, "There are some bone and brass needles, thread, and gimcracks on the table over there. I've to report to Morantz about the trip. Oh, you can give

Iggie the goose leather ball, but let me give her the doll tonight."

"Oh Ronny, I wish you wouldn't call her 'Iggie.' It sounds so common. I'm glad you're not going out again on another task. Yaraine and I miss you terribly when you're gone so long."

Lord Morantz called out, "Come into my study and tell me your tales. My boys and councilor want to hear it all. My clerk can elaborate at the inn tonight, I wager. No dragons, I understand. I don't see any burns or claw marks."

"Sorry Ulric, Arthur, no dragons but plenty of action. Cerdics said he gave you a summary. We went south-east into the borderlands with Wessel. Lots of rumors, bandits, wild beasts and of course monsters. The bandits avoided us once we picked up some armed men from the villages. They faded off into the moors and fens. We hung a few as a warning; only those we caught with evidence or were firmly identified by the constable. As usual, the wild-beast men turned out to be hairy, disheveled hermits or an ascetic monk living in the caves."

"What about the destructive demons?" asked Morantz. "The ones destroying the fields and crops?"

Cerdics spoke up, "Ranulf set us to take turns watching the undisturbed fields. Ordo spotted the marauders with demonic red eyes, tusks, and cloven hooves. We caught one in the act of plowing a field. There will be fresh rib and pork roast for dinner, a   little tough but what can you expect from a demon."

Ranulf continued, "We tracked the other into the moor. He killed a dog and slashed one of the tenants pretty severely. The dents and rents in my armor came when I moved in with a boar spear. Send a servant back in a few weeks to pick out a ham and slabs of bacon. We promised the villagers they could have the rest to offset their lost crops."

"What of the six-and-a-half-foot tall monster that drank all of the taverns mead and tried to break into his cook house?" asked Morantz?

"An old bear, past his prime, scarred and hurting. Ordo and Cerdics dispatched him, a mercy killing considering his condition. His pelt was scarred. We left it with the owner of the inn to make up for the loss of mead."

Ulric and Arthur spoke together, "What of the dragon, the village bailiff reported the Fen dwellers claimed a dragon. They said it ate a dog and dragged off some straying sheep. Yes, and a young goat herder said it charged at him—it had a long tongue and hissed fiercely."

"Let me tell you boys a tale of a beast I had never seen before," began Ranulf. "Cerdics, Ordo, and I went to the area where the beast was last seen. A villager and the very goat header you spoke of led us there. It was out where the fens and swamp lands merge. Watery pathways, soggy ground, bogs giving way to occasional knots or mounds. A weird and dismal place. We dared not venture too far in, the horses were useless, snorted and reared back at the smell."

"Did you see him, was he fierce and scaly, did he breathe fire?" stammered Arthur.

"Well, let me continue after a cup of ale all round. It's a parching subject."

"Go on, go on, please," pleaded Ulric.

Cerdics took up the tale. "Sir Ranulf found this strange, hollowed track, you know, like otters make playing and sliding, but it was on level ground, It had deep claw marks wide apart on the track. You could see and smell where creature stashed its kill to eat later. We found remnants of wool and hair. It must have been in the area for a while."

"Does it eat people? It sounds like a dragon," asked a young page.

Ranulf took over the story, "Well boys, milord, I hate to say it, but we did find evidence that it had taken a young fisherman. We found his fish-spear, wicker basket, signs of struggle and drag marks, also blood. His family had reported him gone, but he often stayed out late. Sorry to say, we were loath to stay there so we retreated to the meadow and dry ground."

Cerdics again continued the tale, "We could hear movement, coughs and grunts, the sounds of feeding unlike any I've heard before. The next day Ordo brought an old sheep carcass, scavenged from a bog, as bait. The animal seems to prefer rotting meat."

"I put it near the trail," said Ordo speaking from the back, "but far enough away that it would have to come for it. By all reports it couldn't fly, so we felt it would crawl out."

Even Morantz was excited now, "You, Scribe, are you getting all this down? I want it transcribed into my journals, for the archives. Go on!"

Ranulf downed his ale and went on, "We went on foot, even Roland was round-eyed and skittish. People from the farms, fens, and village had now come up behind us to see what would happen. A few even carried old pagan amulets as well as their rosaries. The priest took no notice. Those with useful weapons, we directed to cut off its retreat."

"It was an ugly thing, low to the ground but quick. Its tongue was long and thin, it flicked it out as if sensing things. It had a thick, wide body covered with armor like scales, but ridged and wrinkled. More a giant lizard than a dragon. A heavy tail, no spikes, that it moved side to side. No flames breathed out, but a dreadful stench came from its open jaws. It was like the offal pit where the butcher and the scavengers throw the guts and old carcasses of dead animals. It showed no fear, lunging at the men and dogs brave enough to get near. Ordo and a yeoman shot bolts from their crossbows, but they barely penetrated the hide and fell out, doing no damage.

I finally get in close with a woodcutter's axe and severed a leg. Cerdics rushed in on the side and plunged a boar-spear into its neck, while I gave it another blow with the axe. Even then it thrashed and tried to get to the nearest dogs. It finally bled out."

"Did you bring back the beast? I would like to take its dimensions and describe it," said Morantz.

"Ordo has a piece of the hide and the leg I cut off. It weighed as much as an ox and really stank. The villagers cut off its head and stuck it on a stake to scare off thieves. A monk living nearby was a passible artist. He took dimensions, measured it, and made drawings unadorned by fanciful wings, spikes or crests. We brought them back with us."

A week later Lord Morantz returned to the site with a party led by Ordo to view the remains such as they were. Wolves and pigs had worked over the creature, but the tough, thick hide had restricted the damage. The scribe took notes, measured the body, wrote a description and interviewed the monk. Giving the village some coins for the head, Morantz returned to the castle adding the new skull to his collection of oddments. The people came round to see the skull and drawings. Most believing it was a dragon, others clutching holy objects to protect them from of Satan's demons.

Thus began the tales of Ranulf and his stalwart band of dragon slayers. A thousand years later, anthropologists and historians would wonder how the sketches and skull of a Komodo Dragon reached a small castle in the British Midlands.

Bingo at the Senior Clubhouse
By Rita Leitner

"Quiet, please, let's keep it down. This will be a straight Bingo, vertical, horizontal, or four corners."

"Here's our first number...N-33."

"Holy cow, I was born in THAT year. Yep, 1933, F.D.R., the Big Depression was in full swing, and then I showed up!"

"Shush, I can't hear."

"Excuse me."

"N-42."

"How I wish I was forty-two."

"Big deal, you look thirty-seven, so don't complain, my dear."

"G-66."

"I got it."

"So, what?"

"Well, you don't have to be such a pill."

"Who's a pill?"

"Leave the old fart alone, dear, he's building up to his Maalox Moment."

"N-21."

"Ah, yes. I remember…Frankie Sinatra singing to me, 'When I was twenty-one, that was a very good year.'"

"My God, is this 'Name That Tune' or Bingo?"

"Shush."

"B-9."

"Sounds like a tumor to me."

"Speaking of tumors, how's Fred?"

"G-56."

"Oh, you didn't hear? He had prostate surgery."

"Great balls of fire."

"Not anymore."

"Before I say anymore, look who just waltzed in?"

"G-52."

"I suppose that's the year you graduated from high school?"

"Nope, that's the plane George flew in Korea, or was it a B-52?"

"Is that a wig or did the hairdresser experiment again?"

"Let's hope it's a wig. She can hang it up at the end of the day."

"Meow, you old cats."

"I-16."

"How I wish."

"B-7."

"Bingo, yeah, this game's not so bad after all."

"Hold your cards, we have a winner."

"Ah yes, there's good news tonight…we will present a turkey to our next winner."

"Leave it to me to get 'the bird', ah what?"

"Now try not to be so fowl, darling, you're getting down-right grainy, if you catch my drift, Tom."

"You know, I wouldn't want to 'ruffle your feathers,' my sweet little chucky."

"Let the game for the game begin."

"Our first number is O-65."

"Social security, here I come."

"You got to live through tonight, first."

A Caterpillar Sandwich
By Rita Leitner

In the summer of 1965, I had been expecting a baby, but after three weeks of waiting after the due date, Bob and I decided to go camping with our seven kids, aged one to eight years.

We drove up to our property on Mount Umunhum in our VW camper with a trailer. We were camping next to a beautiful mountain river and one morning I was fixing breakfast on the camp fire roasting bacon on a stick when my son Joey came running over in a panic. He had been eating a peanut butter and jelly sandwich and he found a beautiful caterpillar crawling on a plant and picked it up for a closer look. After a few minutes Joey was still hungry, so he took another bite out of the sandwich or so he thought. Suddenly, he noticed a strange sensation on his tongue and realized he hadn't bitten the sandwich, but the caterpillar instead!

"Mommy, mommy! Help! Help!" Joey ran screaming. His tongue was swelling and his stomach was upset since he had accidently swallowed part of the caterpillar. We had to go to the hospital, but before we could leave, we had to pack up all our food and camping gear and all the kids who were freaking out.

Bob started driving way too fast around the winding mountain curves and after the second curve the trailer rolled over. We stopped and had to tip the trailer back over, but it was full of all our camping gear and food and heavy as hell. As it was dangerous being stuck on a narrow mountain road, I kept all the kids in the car, and Bob and I tried the best to tip the trailer back over. After several failed attempts, we finally were able to tip it back upright. However, the strain of lifting and tipping the camper sent me into labor! I thought, "Ee gads! What next?!!!"

Now, Bob was at the end of his rope with a son who has been poisoned, a wife in labor, and six screaming daughters (aged one to eight). We decided to start singing to calm everyone down.

"We're on our way, pack up our packs... and if we stay, we won't be back. How can we go, we haven't got a dime. But we're going and we're gonna' have a happy time!"

Bob began driving more slowly and I began putting cold compresses onto Joey's swollen tongue.

After getting through the extra winding roads we finally made it to the main highway and we figured Dr. Robert Kelley's office in Cupertino was only ten minutes away, but one of the tires on the overloaded trailer blew out and we didn't have a spare! So, we just kept driving. Our poor VW van crept along the busy thoroughfare with cars honking steadily at us and people yelling, "Get off the road, you've got a flat!" In the end, it took us over a half an hour to finally get to the Doc's office.

We all went into the office as a family and begged to get seen immediately. Dr. Kelley tended to Joey and gave him a shot of antibiotics as his tongue had swollen to twice its normal size.

After we got home the labor pains became more frequent, and as soon as I could find a babysitter, (our neighbour, Betty Gordon), we finally went to the hospital to deliver a new baby boy. Tom had finally arrived! Ten pounds, seven ounces, on Flag Day, June 14th 1965.

When I returned home with the newly born Tom, I asked Bob if he wanted to go camping next weekend? His reply was, "Hrrrupmth!"

My Proudest Moment
By Rita Leitner

The bright sun's rays bounced from the '67 Ford's front bumper. This station wagon, with its "woody-textured" panels, was parked forlornly in my driveway. It was registered, insured, and paid for; free and clear. It even had a name, "Herman" (in honor of "Woody" Herman.) There was only one reason Herman sat waiting for me: I did not possess a driver's license.

A mother of eight children, in my mid-thirties, two dogs, a cat, and I could not drive legally. My friends encouraged, cajoled, and instructed me, and finally the day arrived.

The culmination came after weeks of parallel parking in the dark—I waited until the kids were in bed to practice. The Department of Motor Vehicles road test was my chance to prove to the world and myself, that "Herman" and I were safe and legal on the highways and low-ways of beautiful California. Since the six-month probationary period of the Driver's permit was about to expire, I was down to the wire.

I called to make the appointment. Everything was set. My friend Donna baby sat the children. Sue, a dear neighbor, endowed with patience and charity, drove me to the DMV office. I was a whimpering, nervous glob by the time the road test began. The "Inspector General" came limping toward me, as I forced a casual smile his way. I imagined that he had been run into by a woman driver, who had left him bleeding, in the pouring rain, by the deserted road...never again to trust a woman behind the wheel of anything.

This morose male was about to watch me perform...then, ultimately decide whether or not I could own a valid driver's license. Did I feel like a puppet whose strings were about to break? You bet your sweet hubcaps! I decided to pull out all the stops, every feminine trick I could conjure up would be used. The stakes were high. A chance at independence! This was my opportunity to find a new dimension: a free way, via freeways in my future.

I started talking incessantly about the weather, traffic, anything the "General" might find amusing. His reply: "Please be quiet, you're not allowed to talk to the examiner during a test."

I knew I was a goner. He was the world's most insensitive "grouch-with-a-limp." I had no place to run. I was the universe's lowliest creature, and I didn't really think I could pass this test or any test at that moment.

The time went quickly. I didn't hit anyone or anything, as we drove in silence. For the first time in my life, I felt completely powerless. Resigned to the obvious outcome, I asked: "What do I do now?"

He nonchalantly handed me the green sheet he had been marking up, and said, "You passed. Go to counter 'B' and have your picture taken."

I was so high with the thrill of that moment, I floated to Counter B. I was glowing so much, I doubt that a flash was necessary to take the picture. Sue and I stopped by the liquor store and splurged on a bottle of cheap Champagne. I drove "Herman" all the way home.

We gathered the children, neighbors, and postman. All of us celebrated this memorable fete!

It's been 25 years since that awesome event. I still haven't hit anyone or anything. A ticket or two has passed my way, but Traffic School erased them from my slate. In all humility and honesty, I must admit I'm a good, safe, valid California driver. I know the "Inspector General" would be pleased with my record.

My Profiles
By Rita Leitner

Being the first mortician on the scene, just after the Coast Guard had released the bodies, Peter was shocked when he read the ID. A quick check of the files and a look into the body bags confirmed that these were the people he had sailed with just three years ago. He was to have gone this time, but the impending birth of his first child had caused him to cancel the trip.

After taking care of details and notifying families, Peter found the journal he had made on that trip. He was dog tired but couldn't sleep until he read to the last word.

Mary Lou Peterson's flirtatious blue eyes, well-coiffured auburn tresses, and stately countenance gave no clue to the real turmoil within her psyche. Third in a family of five, she was the invisible child. Now, at thirty-two, the inner child was screaming to get out, to get even at those years of fear and malevolence. An external masquerade was to be revealed. The behavior so cleverly squelched by this imposter, will be replaced by one of rage and hysteria.

Mary Lou is in crisis. She is choosing to act, not react, to life's experiences.

Bob Carlton aka "Pookie" is everyone's little brother. Always ready with a quick smile. He illuminated the surroundings with his presence. A top-notch basketball player, he is eager to participate in any competition, verbal or physical. He gives his best: wins with grace, loses with finesse. Handsome and virile, he possesses the three "S's" namely: sensibility, sensitivity and sensuality. "Pookie" is popular with both genders. Fun to be around, he is rarely alone. He likes it that way. "He is a people person," everyone happily admits.

Gail Hemingway, aloof or just quiet? Her majestic stature gives one the feeling that this lady has royal blood from some past life from "jolly olde England" bubbling in her varicose veins. For fifty-some years this matriarch has silently permeated the family scene with her regal elegance. Her dark brown, peering gaze brings new meaning to the old adage: "Eyes are the window to the soul."

One heart operation, a kidney removal, and various ailments in the gastro-intestinal area, have left Gail no worse off than most of her senior contemporaries. Grandmother to six adorable "ragamuffins," as she so tenderly refers to her growing brood, Gail tries to let their parents raise them, wisely staying in the background whenever possible. At five feet, ten inches, that is difficult to do on most occasions, but Granny Gail manages quite well.

High Tech job, yuppy associates, BMW with cellular car phone, state-of-the-art high-profile lifestyle: that's Diane DeWree, trying to pluck the golden fruit from the tree in the Fortune 500 Orchard.

Well-educated in the middle-class system, Diane graduated *Magna Cum Laude*, earning a master's degree in Business Ad. She is the pride and joy of her parents, friends, and associates. Yet, something is missing in her life. Could it be a commitment to someone special? Is the AIDS scare keeping her from a meaningful relationship? Is AIDS just a great excuse for running faster to reach yet another goal at work? Where does it end? Diane is twenty-nine: next year will be the BIG ONE. It is time to get to the real meaning of this existence on earth before life becomes "Garbage in, Garbage Out."

Penny Nicholson loves to sing. At thirty-nine, divorced, mother of two teenagers, single parenting is a challenge, to say the least. She feels she deserves a night out, singing with the Sweet Adelines (Lady Barbershop Quartette) so, life is good at last.

Perseverance pays, it wasn't always this easy for Penny. Born in a small town in mid-eastern Texas, life was difficult. Caring, hardworking parents instilled a sense of belonging to the world through nature and its symbiotic relationship to all things. This slight, blonde, vivacious mom had learned her life-lessons well, to accentuate the positive...eliminate the negative, became standard procedure for this fair lady.

What's a Mother For?
By Rita Leitner

The autumn leaves were gently falling: the crisp air gave exuberance to each activity. The wedding plans were set; Saturday morning, eleven, in a sweet Los Altos church, very romantically nestled in the woods. Joan, the bride, was the most organized of the six girls and two boys in the family.

The rehearsal was scheduled for tonight, Friday, October 13th. A dinner for the bridal party was to follow at a favorite Italian restaurant.

Weekend guests had been picked up from the airport, as arranged. Needless to say, the place was jumping with energy and enthusiasm. It was six p.m.

I shall never forget the frantic squeal from Mary, the eldest, emanating from the front bathroom! Dead silence filled the living room. Mary announced to the anxious bride: "The toilet is backing up, overflowing, and gushing out the bathtub!"

After a quick check, the plumbing problem was simultaneously occurring in every sink in the house, kitchen and three bathrooms, all showers included. The diagnosis: the septic tank was filled to capacity; therefore, all excessive materials were regurgitating mercilessly through the house's sewage system.

What's a mother to do?

After several unpolluted deep breaths taken from the front porch, I calmed down the some-crying, some-laughing conglomerate of humanity, noting the "fine line" between comedy and tragedy. I headed for the yellow pages of the phone book to supply me with options.

I settled for a 24-hour emergency septic tank repair service called "Able Septic Speedy Service," guaranteed to pump your sump. This sounded good to me. I called immediately, the truck promised to show up "ASAP" or whatever THAT was.

The bridal party took off for rehearsal, while I prepared for the Septic man. A neighbor called to see if she could help with any last-minute wedding chores. She was shocked to hear of the volcano eruptions in our plumbing, and generously offered to take my house guests for the night. I called another neighbor to arrange for the bride and the bridesmaids. What would we do without friends and neighbors?

The septic company arrived. He did his emergency pumping for a mere $100.00. After further examination he quoted $3,500 for new leach lines and another septic tank to be dug in the very near future. This was not what I hoped to hear. For now, our main concern was 250 guests due at 11 a.m. tomorrow. We had a wedding to "enjoy..." so, I wrote a check to the septic serviceman, cleaned up the sinks, sprayed Lysol disinfectant over everything in sight, got dressed, drank wine, ate garlic bread, and laughed until I cried. Fine time had by all.

Joan's wedding was the social event of the season. Unfortunately, the marriage did not last as long as the new septic tank. Perhaps the backed-up plumbing was an omen on Friday the thirteenth.

Just Call Me "Dave"
By Chuck Northup

The news was headlines: 230 lost at sea. The Equatorial Eagle Airline jet went down in the Gulf of Mexico with all on board. Cause is still unknown. The jet was on a flight from Chicago to Quito,

The airline was known as the Double Eagle because of its name, and made flights into the Southern Hemisphere several times daily. It was famous for its ritual when crossing the equator. Everyone got a free drink and a certificate making them Shellbacks (Quito is above the equator, so no such ritual occurred on this flight.)

When he read the news, Dave was devastated. His soon to-be-bride was on that flight. He and Johanna were in their last year at Northwestern University, and were to be married in the month following their graduation. Johanna was making a quick trip to visit her father who was an executive in the recently acquired Heineken brewery in Quito, Ecuador. Dave was beside himself and quit all his classes because he couldn't think of studying during his grief.

I was headed for the Home Depot, but stuck at the light at the corner of N. Elston Ave. and N. Magnolia Ave. in Chicago, and I saw a man standing on the corner with a sign saying "Will work for food." He was a husky looking young man, probably in his mid-20s, and seemed as though he could do a good days work, so I rolled down the passenger window and called him over.

"I need some shelving put up in my home. Can you do that kind of work?"

"I sure can," he replied.

"Get in. I'm going to Home Depot to pick up material. My name is Jake Wellsby. What's yours?"

"Just call me 'Dave,'" he said. "I can do all kinds of carpentry."

"That's good to know. Where'd you get your experience?" I asked.

"I was born and raised on a farm in Iowa. We had to do all kinds of work to keep the place going. We never hired anyone—my brother and I did everything ourselves. You get lots of experience that way."

"That's wonderful. I have a small ranch nearby, and I have a lot of small jobs to do. Have you got some extra time?" I asked, hoping I could get a good handyman.

"Sure. I've got plenty of time right now. How far away do you live?" Dave asked.

"I have a place in Wayne, about 35 miles west of here. I came into town on business and needed to get some stuff for the shelving. It'll probably take you a couple of days to do the work. I have a small cottage on the grounds for you to stay in. Can you stay that long?"

"No problem," Dave answered. "I'm not doing anything right now."

We stopped at the Home Depot and picked up shelving, brackets, hinges, cabinet doors, and some handles.

"Do you have plenty of nails?" Dave asked.

"Good question," I said, "we should get some now, and we need screws for the hinges and handles, too."

"Do you want these shelves painted?" Dave asked.

"I hadn't thought of that, but it would be a good idea. We can pick up some paint as well," I answered.

Dave didn't talk much on the way to my ranch, but he commented about all the horses around Wayne. I didn't want to question him about his   private life. I introduced him to my wife Beth, and she told us to sit down to lunch— she had just finished making a nice salad, sandwiches, and iced tea along with an apple pie.

I told Beth, "I hired Dave to set up the shelving in my office. I told him he could use the back cottage to sleep overnight."

"I'll get fresh sheets and make the bed," said Beth.

After lunch, I showed Dave where I wanted the cabinets and shelving in a large closet in my home   office. He went right to work, obviously knowing   exactly what to do. I was pleased that I had made a good choice just picking him off the street.

I had carefully saved the glass Dave had used at lunch, and using a phone out of hearing of Dave, I called the security manager of my company in Chicago.

"Harry, I've just hired a stranger to do some work at my ranch. He won't tell me his last name, but I have his fingerprints on a glass he used. I'd like you to pick up this glass and investigate him as soon as you can. Can you do that today?"

"Yes," Harry answered. "I'll be there in about an hour or so."

"Good," I said. "I don't want to harbor a murderer or rapist—see you soon."

"Okay," Harry said. "With the weekend coming on though, I won't be able to get answers before Monday or Tuesday." He hung up.

Dave was doing well with the shelf and cabinet work in the closet behind me, while I worked on my computer nearby. Every now and then, I would check to see how he was coming along. We had a coffee break in the afternoon and dinner later. I invited him to watch TV with us in the living room that evening, but he said he preferred to be alone, and went to the cottage out back. He was up and ready in the morning.

At breakfast he said, "Your bed is very comfortable; I had a good rest last night. It's really quiet out here, but I did hear some horses this morning."

Dave spoke more at breakfast, but nothing personal. He talked about my ranch and the surrounding area. He liked my house, but asked nothing of our personal life, and we didn't ask about his. We went back to work in my office.

I sometimes swear at my computer when it does something I don't like.

I shouted, "God damn it!"

That brought Dave out to stand behind me looking over my shoulder.

He asked, "What's wrong?"

I said, "The answer won't come out right."

He looked at my screen for a few moments, and then said to me, "You've got the formula wrong. You've got to have x over y, not y over x."

I looked at him in amazement. "How'd you know that?" I asked.

"Oh, I learned that in school," he answered.

I knew that this was not learned in ordinary algebra. This was very advanced calculus.

"Thank you," I said. "I've only been fighting this for 15 minutes."

I corrected the formula and got my answer. Dave continued his cabinetry.

As the afternoon got late, I told Dave to stop for the day. After dinner, he agreed to stay with us to watch TV, then took off to bed.

When Monday came, I went into Chicago to my office. Mid-morning, Harry came to me and said, "I just got a report on your stranger. You'll be okay with him. You've got a really smart guy on your hands."

Harry handed me a folder with a one-page report complete with photo. It contained the following information:

This report was not gathered from police records—there were none. It was found because David attended Northwestern University which took photos and fingerprints upon entry. They were sent to the FBI where records are kept in their *History* Summary *Check* for noncriminal justice purposes.

"Dave's name is David Jansen. He graduated *Summa cum laude*, and is in his last year pursuing a Ph.D. in physics, writing his thesis on quantum mechanics. He was born and raised in Pella, IA, and left his family home to attend Northwestern. He has no arrests or convictions of any kind—not even speeding or parking violations. He was recently engaged to be married to a lady named Johanna de Vries, also from his hometown, but she was in that jet that went down in the Gulf of Mexico a couple of weeks ago.

"He lived with his widowed father and brother who operate a large corn acreage that has been in the family for several generations. David is the first to seek a Ph.D. in the family, although his father and mother were well-educated. He has one other brother and no sisters—none of whom has any police records.

"Johanna de Fries is in the Art History Ph.D. program at Northwestern. She was writing her dissertation on Mid-western U.S. Indian tribal Art, and planned to be a college professor. Her father is an executive with Heineken Brewery in Quito, Ecuador where the corporation recently purchased a brewery, and he now lives alone. Johanna has two other grown, unmarried sisters living in Pella.

"Both David and Johanna are 27 at this date.

"David's counsellor reported that David was completely broken up by Johanna's death and requested a leave of absence from his doctoral studies—which was granted. He deserted his off-campus housing, and it is not known where he now is.

"You have apparently found him. "

Dave finished his work and painting in the closet that day. He had done a fine job, and I complimented him on it.

He asked, "The paint won't be dry until tomorrow; what do you want me to do next?"

"Sit down, Dave," I said quietly.

He sat at my extra chair at my desk.

"Dave," I said, "I own a corporation in Chicago called Compro—you may have heard of it."

He nodded as I spoke.

I continued, "Because of my position, I am vulnerable to dangerous people who want to do me in. I must be very careful of those whom I meet. I hope you don't take this the wrong way, but I had the fingerprints you left on a glass checked by my security department, and I found out all I needed to know about you. You certainly have a fine record!"

"Thank you," said Dave.

"You are far more than a handyman. I was astounded by the way you picked up on my computer error. That formula is one used only in advanced physics. You have the kind of mind that I seek in my employees. I am prepared to offer you a fine job with my corporation if you will consider it. When you finish school, you can come to work immediately, if you desire.

"I'm aware of your terrible loss, and if you wish more grieving time, I will grant it—with pay. I will also pay for your continuance at Northwestern until you graduate. I hope you will consider my offer."

Dave answered, "I'm not angry that you had me investigated—I understand your position. I will consider your offer."

I said, "Dave, "I'd like to take you to my company in Chicago and show you around, so you can get a feel of what we do."

"That's funny," Dave said. "I investigated *your* company already. I know what you do, and I was planning to seek work there, but I would like to look inside, anyway."

Jake drove Dave back to his off-campus apartment for a change of clothes, and then to the corporate headquarters of Compro where Jake showed Dave around and introduced him to various executives, finishing up in the executive dining room with lunch.

I told Dave, "These people in this room all earn high six-and-seven-figure salaries. You could be among them with that head you have on your shoulders.

"By the way, why were you standing on a street corner with that sign?"

Dave answered, "I needed to get away from my studies for a while. I felt that if I could use my muscles instead of my head, I might get over my love loss more quickly. Working at your ranch did that for me, and I thank you for the opportunity."

Epilogue

The next year, Dave resumed his Ph.D. studies and graduated as Valedictorian. He married Johanna's younger sister after graduation.

Meanwhile, his father had died, leaving the family ranch to him and his brother. They were not interested in corn farming, so they sold the huge acreage for $57 million to a tulip bulb company that planned large growing fields and company headquarters for their world-wide operations.

Dave and his nearly-equally intelligent brother started a competing company to Jake's Compro called Image which soon out-paced them. Image bought the struggling company and folded the two operations together in Chicago.

Bowstring
By Chuck Northup

The three fingers on my right hand are aching as they hold the bowstring taut, waiting for the exact moment when the deer turns into the perfect position for my best shot. All is silent but the quiet gurgle of a nearby brook meandering through the rocks of the streambed surrounded by deep, dark woods.

I've walked a couple of miles along a dirt road lined with rattlesnake weed nestled out of the way of tires with their redundancy of mustard-colored flowers decorating the edge of this backwoods trail.

I've found what appears to be an animal trail leading through the thick woods, and hope to possibly see a deer to enhance my food locker. I locate a fairly good hiding place near the trail with a clear view of a sparse opening in the shrubbery for me to get a clean shot.

I am concealed from sight so the deer will not see me, but my crouching makes my knees grow weary and my legs ache. My insides are telling me that I should have relieved myself sooner, but waiting for an animal to appear is a waiting game. I hope that I have found a trail used by the wild ones to seek water.

After hours of crouching, I am rewarded by the sight of a six-point white-tail deer walking slowly toward the brook. He meanders through the tangle of bushes following a trail only he can see. The overhanging tree limbs guard him from his predators and me, but I catch glimpses of him as he travels along his route. There is a slight clearing ahead of him, and when he reaches it, he pauses to look about—maybe to see a tender morsel to eat from a nearby flowering dogwood, now in their blooming season, with their low spreading branches and distinctive white flowers that bring a dead winter forest back to life in the spring.

It is then that I draw back my bow string and take aim and hold it waiting for that perfect moment. But the deer at his transitory rest faces away from my aim, making for a poor target. I must wait until he is broadside for my best chance of hitting a vital organ to cause nearly instant death. The deer is always concerned about predators. He cannot see me, but perhaps he hears or smells my presence. Does he face the wrong way purposely? Does he keep on the move—starting and stopping often? Is he acting by instinct, or does the wary animal consciously know all that information?

It seems that he does, because he remains in this poor posture, nibbling away at the dogwood, seemingly unaware of my presence and my aching arms and fingers that may tire and make a poor shot. Fortunately, I am in a shady spot, well camouflaged by my hunting outfit and the surrounding foliage. My arrow is darkened so that it will not cause a glint of light that might scare my prey.

But when will he turn into position?

My fingers grow even more cramped, and my bladder is now shouting. Will I be able to release the bowstring at the right moment? I dare not try to   relieve the tension for fear of missing the moment for my shot, even though my hand begins to quiver slightly.

He's beginning to turn. My hopes grow. His head rises to an alert position. What did he hear? He certainly did not hear me. I haven't moved a muscle for the long minutes that he has been quietly   munching away on his lunch of tasty new leaves of his favorite dogwood. My bow is bent into its farthest arch to drive a powerful thrusting arrow into my prey in hopes that it will continue through his body and emerge from the other side to produce a sufficient trail of blood for me to track but that arching bow has tired my arm during my wait for the deer to reposition himself.

Suddenly, a covey of quail noisily flutters from a nearby patch of low bushes as they hurriedly rise into the air. The deer is startled momentarily, and takes a few steps back the way he came, ruining my proposed shot. I too, rise to ease the pain in my tired legs and take a few moments to relieve myself—and what a relief it is!

I wait another half-hour for a deer to use the same path, but none appear. During that period, I visualize that beautiful rack I missed, hanging on the wall above my fireplace.

Feeling greatly disappointed, I stop by the butcher on the way home and pick up a pound of hamburger.

Flapping Tongues -1
By Chuck Northup

Nora and her daughter were held at the stop light when a speeding car came up from behind, ignored the light, and crashed into the rear of their car. Nora heard the brakes at the last moment, glanced into the rear-view mirror, and saw the fast-approaching headlights near her bumper, but she could do nothing but brace herself against the back of her seat and throw her arm in front of her daughter. There was a car in front of her, so the crash involved that car as well. She was sandwiched between the stopped car in front of her and the onrushing vehicle behind. She had just refilled her gas tank, and it was the first to receive the force, so there was a huge explosion, killing the reckless driver, Nora, her daughter, and severely injuring the driver of the forward car who barely escaped with his life.

"I can handle my own dinner tonight," said Harry.

"Well, the last time you used the microwave for popcorn, you burned it."

"There are a couple of TV dinners in the fridge. Choose the one you like and read the directions. Try not to burn it," said Nora as she bustled around the kitchen gathering up the things she needed for the Mother and Daughter Dinner at the church a few miles away—they had recently changed churches because they didn't care for the new minister at the close-by church.

"I know how to use the microwave, and the popcorn burned, if you remember, because we were too busy making out on the living room couch."

Harry and Nora had been sweethearts since high school. He was perhaps the handsomest young man in school, and all the girls wanted to date him. He had to fight them off like flies. Nora was the winner, and after living together a couple of years and attending college, Nora became pregnant. Their marriage was attended by everyone they knew, and their union remained happy throughout seven years and birth of Jennifer.

"Jennifer!" Nora called. "Are you ready to go?"

"I'm just getting my jacket—I'm ready."

Out the door they went and into Nora's car. Nora glanced at the gas gauge riding on empty.

"I'd better stop for gas. I don't want to run out before we get back home."

Harry finished his TV dinner and was working on a set of books he had brought home. He worked for an accounting firm that took in work from about a 50-mile circle. Harry's specialty was florist shops. He took care of perhaps a dozen or more from the surrounding area.

He gained the capability of determining the reasons for the rise and fall of profit of various shops just by doing their books. He could tell when inept purchases were made or when certain bouquets were underpriced or overpriced. Because of his expertise, he was an asset to his firm, and most florists used the firm's services because of him.

The phone rang, and Harry picked it up. "Is Nora on the way?" asked a worried voice.

"Well—yes." Harry said hesitantly. "She left some time ago. She must have gotten tied up in traffic.

The call was interrupted by the doorbell.

"There's someone at the door—just a moment."

Harry set the phone down on the table and went to the door. The person on the phone could clearly hear Harry and his visitor.

"Mr. Gunderson?"

"Yes."

"I am Detective Potter with the police department. I have some very sad news to tell you. May I come in?"

"Of course, please come in. Is this about my wife and daughter?" asked Harry hesitantly.

The two men went into the living room and sat down. The policeman carefully related to Harry the story of the accident caused by a drunken driver. Arrangements were made for Harry to come down to the coroner's office the next day.

It was several weeks before Harry was able to act normally again. Meanwhile, he moved around like a robot in the office.

One day, he was speaking to a florist client who had several branch shops. Harry had been working with him for many years.

"Harry, I wish to express my sympathy for your great loss. To put your mind into a different state, I have a proposition for you to consider. You've been doing our books for so long that you know our business well. Would you like a full-time job at our company as our chief accountant?"

The client named a salary that was well above what Harry was presently earning, and Harry knew that the florist was on good footing, so he answered in the affirmative.

"Then why not come down this weekend and we can work out the details."

The florist was located in a nearby small town, but it was very successful. However, Harry had noticed that recently the profits had fallen somewhat, and thought he might be able to shore them up if he worked there. When he arrived at the store the following Sunday, he found out why things had changed—the client's partner had died.

"Harry," before you agree to work for me, there's something you should know. I'm openly gay, and the whole town knows it. My late partner and I were married and operating this shop together. Since he passed away, things have not been going so well. He did the back-room work, and I worked up front. He couldn't handle customers well, and I didn't know how to order well. I've got to replace him, but in addition, our company has grown so large, we need to do our accounting on-site."

Harry interrupted, "I'm sorry for your loss as well. I've noticed the drop in profit, and I don't care about your private life."

Germaine, the florist, replied, "I'm telling you this because the people in this town are gossips. I'm sure they saw you come in with me today when we're closed, and the tongues will start wagging. You will bear the brunt of the suspicions. They'll probably consider you gay also, especially later when you are often seen with me."

And right he was!

Standing in line at the grocery store one lady said to another, "Did you see that nice handsome man going into the florist shop with Germaine on the weekend?"

"Yes, I did. Germaine is so lonely since his partner died, you can surmise what they were doing in there on Sunday."

"He's probably Germaine's new boyfriend, now that his partner is dead. Why are gay guys always so handsome?"

At a local bar, two guys on stools were talking.

"Did you see that new guy hanging around the florist shop? He's there all the time."

"Yeah, Germaine needs a new lover, ya' know, and I sure don't want him around me!"

"You won't have to worry—you sure ain't as cute as that new guy!"

Tongues were flying faster than a hummingbird's wings all over town, and word got back to Germaine. He decided he would do something about it.

The next time when the town's biggest gossip came into the shop, Germaine approached her and said, "Maggie, I'd like you to meet someone."

Germaine picked up the intercom and called Harry down to the cashier's stand. While he was coming, Germaine explained that Harry was his new chief accountant replacing his late partner in that job. Harry had been doing the company's books while working at an accountant's office in the nearby city. Germaine further explained that Harry had recently lost his wife and daughter in a horrendous auto accident and needed a change in scenery.

That did the trick. Maggie spread the word. Harry had had a wife and child; therefore, he probably was not gay, but that was never a sure thing. However, his change from doing the florist's books in a different city and moving to a local place made good sense. The two men being seen together was also natural because Germaine did need a back-shop person to replace his former partner.

Almost overnight, Harry started getting invitations to gatherings and dinners at people's homes—many to introduce their available daughters—after all, he was still a handsome, available, 27-year-old straight bachelor.

Flapping Tongues - 2
By Chuck Northup

"Honey," said Terry as he came in the back door stamping his feet to get the mud off his shoes, "I've got bad news for you."

"Yeah, I already know," said Lorraine, "Grover Cleveland dug a hole in my pansy bed. I saw it yesterday—he must have been after that gopher we've got in the garden."

Rover was too common, so they called him Grover, and the only Grover they knew about was the former president, so the dog's name became Grover Cleveland, a truly elegant name for a black Labrador.

"No, it's worse than that. During the storm last night, I heard a crash, so this morning I went out to see what it was. You know that beautiful flowering crabapple tree we planted a couple of years ago to shade the dog house? Well, that wind we had last night pulled it right out of the ground by the roots, and blew it down onto Grover's house and smashed it. Grover will have to sleep somewhere else until I can get it fixed."

She answered, "Oh my gosh! That's terrible. It was such a gorgeous tree when it bloomed last year, and it was just getting ready to bloom again."

Terry muttered, "We probably should have bought a smaller tree so it could get its roots into the ground better."

Lorraine said, "Remember, we talked about that at the nursery. And we opted for the big one so we would get blooms right away."

"I guess we were too impatient," said Terry. "Now we're paying the price—we'll just have to buy another one."

"Stop worrying about it—sit down and eat your breakfast. I fixed your favorite cheese and onion omelet and hash browns," said Lorraine.

"Those sausages look good, too." said Terry as he slid into his chair, opened the newspaper, and grabbed his napkin.

"What plans do you have for today?" asked Lorraine, as she buttered some toast.

"After my walk, I think I'll check out what I need in order to fix the dog house, and then go down to the hardware store for new material. Building a new one will take most of the day. What are your plans?"

"I'm going to fill in that hole Grover made. Maybe, if you've got the time, we could stop by the nursery, pick up a new tree, and get some pansies to replace the ones Grover ruined. Maybe we could get a gopher trap to catch that little devil who's been eating my pansies."

Terry folded the paper, wiped his mouth, and said, "That was a delicious breakfast. Right now, I'm going to take a walk and get rid of some of those calories you fed me. I'll see you in a while."

Terry had a favorite route that he liked to follow for his two-mile walk. He headed for the nearby park that had a small lake he enjoyed. Last night's storm had brought down several limbs from trees surrounding the lake, but crews were already busy cleaning things up, so the public could use the park. Spring was not far off, and most trees were adding new greenery to their shapes.

Terry was happy to see that the daffodils were starting to bloom where the landscapers had planted them along the walkways. Their huge yellow blossoms were outstanding and brought a lot of color to the park. The tiny lake had a few mallard ducks—the males with their bright colors and the females in drab feathers alongside their mates. Terry heard the quacking of the romancing males. While walking along the trees and flowering bulbs, he had no idea of what lay ahead for him.

He was coming to the portion of his walk that he did not enjoy, but couldn't avoid—the short part that was along the busy main road. There was lots of   traffic that Saturday as usual, and the stench of exhaust bothered Terry. He couldn't wait until he would be back into the inner walkways of the park and breathe the fresh air filtered by the greenery.

Suddenly, he heard a screeching of tires on the moist pavement. He looked up just in time to see a large truck in the eastbound lane cross over into the westbound lane and crash headlong into a car. Traffic was moving steadily at about 50 m.p.h. in both directions, so the collision between the truck and car had the force of about 100 m.p.h. at the time of impact.

The accident was not over 20 feet directly in front of Terry, and he saw the entire gruesome carnage. The large truck made an accordion fold of the front of the car. The two adults in the front seat were crushed by the dashboard and windshield. It was obvious that they were killed instantly. All the doors of the car were forced open by the sudden halt. But there was a weird momentary quiet as all traffic stopped and the horns quieted.

Terry heard the crying of a baby, and looked at the open back seat of the car to see a baby seat with a tiny child strapped into it. The child was probably less than a year old and crying loudly.

Fearing the car might catch fire, Terry ran the few steps to the car, reached into the back seat, unharnessed the baby and lifted him out of the seat. Terry hugged the child and ran back to the sidewalk, just as the car burst into flame.

Terry moved farther away from the heat and soothed the baby boy until he stopped crying. Terry did not want the child to watch his parents burning—he huddled the baby's head into his chest and went further into the park. Sirens were heard and firemen were soon dousing the fire.

Terry walked over to one of the ambulance attendants and handed the child to him, saying, "This boy was in the back seat of the car. I took him out before the fire."

"Please wait here," said the attendant. "The police will want your statement."

Terry found a nearby bench and waited until the police spoke to him and got his first-hand account of the accident. Terry continued to his home.

Terry did not want to upset his wife with the story about the accident, so as he came into the house, he said, "Lorrie, I think I'll hold off on rebuilding the dog house. Instead, let's go down to the nursery now and get the new plants. That way, you'll have time to plant your flowers, and I can get the new tree into the ground. Mr. Cleveland can sleep on the back porch for a while."

The Sunday morning paper had the headline: PASSERBY SAVES BABY, with a full account of the collision, including Terry's name. The article told of the bravery and quick thinking of Terry, but it also told of the sad deaths, the cremating of the baby's parents, and how Terry had shielded the baby from viewing it. The accident was caused by a tire blowout on the left front of the truck, causing it to veer into the opposing lane of traffic.

Terry buried the paper in a pile of old newspapers. Lorraine never saw the article. She heard of her husband's heroic action from neighbors, and was thrilled by the news. She went right home and baked a cake. That night at dinner, she presented the cake.

"What's this for?" said Terry.

"Take a look," said Lorraine.

On the cake printed in bold frosting was "HERO."

When you go to the store, do you intentionally buy something weird?

Pal
By Chuck Northup

When you go to the store, do you intentionally buy something weird?

Well, neither did we, but that seems to be what happened.

My brother and I lived together, and one day we decided to get a pet to add to our lonely existence. We had no idea that a pet could do so much to entertain us, but we soon found out.

We went to a local pet shop and saw many dogs that were nice looking in pens. It was difficult for us to choose one, so the owner of the shop asked us questions.

"How big a dog do you want?"

I answered, "Not too big—I don't want to feed a great big dog that will eat us out of house and home."

"How tall do you think you'd like him to be?"

My brother, Ted, answered him by putting his hand about 18 inches above the floor saying, "No   bigger than this."

"Is that his head or his shoulder height? His head would add about 8 or 10 inches to that measure."

"That would be too big," I said "Let's make that the top of his head."

The owner took us down an aisle and pointed out some smaller puppies.

"Any of these would grow to the size you want," he said.

All of the puppies were busy doing something, but one came to the front of the cage and looked at us. I reached down, and the puppy licked my hand.

"This is the one," I said. "What kind is it?"

The owner said he didn't know—it was just a mixed breed, but he could tell that it wouldn't grow too large.

Ted agreed that it was an okay puppy.

We got the works—bed, blanket, food tray, food, some toys, and a collar with leash. I imagine the store owner was happy with us—and we were happy with our purchase, so home we went. We decided to call him "Pal" because he would now be our pal.

We had a house with a back yard, so Pal would run around and play outside. We cut a dog door into the back door so Pal could run out whenever he wished. We hung a ribboned curtain over the door to keep the wind out and taught Pal how to go through it, which he quickly learned.

Pal grew up to be the size we expected, and he couldn't choose who to sleep with, so he slept part of the time with me and part of the time with Ted. He used his dog bed only during the day and always slept with us at night.

Our lives were somewhat dull. At night we watched TV—I say "we" including Pal. He would watch intently, but he especially liked certain things, such as horses and ducks. Whenever one of those appeared on the screen, Pal would sit up or jump down to the front of the TV to watch more closely. One thing he did all the time was to bark when the theme song for *Law and Order* came on. No other song excited him—only that one. He would jump down and turn circles in front of the TV when that theme played. Who knows why?

He enjoyed taking walks, and would get his leash by taking it off the doorknob where we hung it, and bringing it to us when he wanted to go for a walk. When we returned from our walk,

I would leave the leash on his collar because Pal liked to go around the kitchen central pedestal following his lease around. He would go round and round until he finally got tired and lay down. It was weird to watch him doing it, and he often continued for 15 minutes.

Ted wore a partial toupee, and Pal loved to sneak up behind the chair Ted was sitting in, grab his toupee off his head, and run into the bedroom with it. He knew that Ted would follow him and catch him which he really loved.

For fun we would sometimes give Pal a big stick and tell him to go outside. Pal would attempt to go through the dog door, but the stick would prevent him. Pal would try and try, then finally drop the stick, go outside, reach back in to pick up the stick, and repeat the same maneuver from the outside. He never could figure out any way to get the stick outside.

Occasionally Pal would discover that he had a tail. He would chase it by going around in one spot, while we laughed. I believe he did it just to make us laugh.

One day, we took a steak out of the freezer and left it on the kitchen counter to thaw. Pal found it, grabbed it, and ran off down the hall.

We had to chase him to save our supper. From then on, we always left frozen meat to thaw on top of the fridge or in the cold oven.

Two guys living together sometimes didn't flush—ostensibly to save water, but one day we caught Pal drinking from the toilet, so we always flushed from then on.

Pal also liked to drag our socks out of the dirty laundry and chew on one. He never made holes in any of them—he just liked the flavor of us.

Another of his favorite enjoyments was riding in the back seat of the car. We would sometimes leave the window down so Pal could stick his head out and let his ears flap and his tongue catch the air, but he liked it best when it rained, because we would let him sit in the front seat when we went alone. Pal would put his paws upon the dashboard and try to catch the windshield wiper as it swished back and forth across the window.

Pal lived to a ripe old age of 18, and when he passed on, we dug a grave for him in the back garden. We even fashioned a coffin out of a small wooden box and lined it with padded cloth. We bought a hybrid rose called John Paul

II—the closest we could get to the spelling of Pal—and planted it over his coffin. The rose blooms from late spring to late summer and produces beautiful white, fragrant roses that we can bring inside to remind us of Pal.

We couldn't get another pet right away. We missed his sitting on our feet while we watched TV, anxiously waiting for something to grab as it "accidentally" dropped from the dinner table, licking our dangling hand when we were asleep in a chair, barking at the TV, and all the other weird stuff he did. We simply wanted to retain the memories of Pal.

Deep in the Heart of Texas
Bye Maya Torngren

When my daughter and her family moved from Alaska to Texas, their two daughters became very much involved in the weather in the two states. They were used to being cold outside and hot inside. Coming to Texas, the very opposite happened--they were hot outside and cold inside.

Texans are very proud of their state. I remember talking to the owner of a small restaurant. She asked me, Susie, and another woman where we were from. We told her that I was from California, via Germany, my daughter was from Alaska, and the other woman from Garnish, a beautiful town in Germany. She told us that Texas was more beautiful than anywhere in the world. This happened in West Texas, which isn't really famous for its beauty. But, of course, beauty is in the eyes of the beholder.

If you stay in Texas for any length of time, count on gaining some weight. The food is great everywhere, from the fancy restaurants to the smallest barbecue or Tex-Mex Restaurant. One time my daughter took us to a famous steak house outside of Austin. We all ordered steak and the specialty of the house, which was French fried onion rings. These were served on a big platter, piled high like a hay stack, and were they delicious! When the steaks were served, everybody was happy with their meal except for me. My steak was tough. I wasn't going to say anything, but when the waitress came around asking how everything was, she could tell that I wasn't too happy. She asked me what was wrong, and I told her that my steak was tough. She almost snatched the plate from me and took it to the kitchen and came back with another steak for me.

This was the best most tender steak I had ever eaten and that is true to this day. I guess they couldn't afford to have any unhappy diners.

Toby and I made several small trips to Texas hill country. Of course these weren't considered hills by Alaska, Bavaria, or California standards, but they were gently rolling hills, dotted with small towns, and wildflowers everywhere. We stopped at a small restaurant to have lunch in one of those places. They offered dinner with a drink and dessert included. The dessert happened to be pie. When I asked the waitress what kind of pie they had, she came up with a card that she recited. I have heard of 25 flavors of ice cream, but I had never heard of 25 different kinds of pie. It was a real hard choice to make.

If you happen to be in Austin between March and October, you have to watch the nature spectacle under the Congress Bridge in Austin. We walked down the path to the banks of the river at dusk. We didn't have to wait very long before we saw a few bats emerging from under the bridge. Then, all of a sudden, thousands of bats could be seen flying out from under the bridge on their way to their evening meal. It was quite a sight to see.

Texas is, politically speaking, a red state. However, it hasn't always been that way. When Texas-born Lyndon B. Johnson was president of the United States, he left quite a formidable domestic legacy, including: the signing of The Civil Rights Act, The Voting Rights Act, Medicare, Medicaid, The Clean Air Act, The Clean Water Act, and many more. His wife, Lady Bird Johnson, left her own legacy by beautifying Texas. You can still see wildflowers everywhere: along freeways and highways, in meadows, wherever they can survive. She was responsible for this beauty, and Texans and the rest of us thank her for it.

Unfortunately, Lyndon Johnson is mostly remembered for the terrible war in Vietnam, overshadowing all his other accomplishments.

Everything is big in Texas. The people are friendly and the weather is hot and humid. I could never get used to it. I guess I prefer the dry heat in California's San Joaquin valley.

Section Three
Owen in America
By Kent Humpal

Last, but not least, one of our members (Kent Humpal) wanted to write a very long and very complete story, which is included here under the above Section Name.

The captain had used sails moving north from San Pedro, but when they turned into the Gate, the outgoing tide, plus the current through the straits, made him shift to the engine.

Owen volunteered to shovel coal to get things moving, and after an hour plus, a pilot boat came out to guide them into a side wharf in Oakland.

"Here's where you get off, Bub. Thanks for the help. You more than paid for your passage. You must have been a sailor at one time," the skipper said.

Owen replied, "I haven't helped set a sail or handle ropes for a few years, but you never forget how, I guess. I jumped ship five years ago when we anchored in Boston. Done a little of everything since."

The first mate and a seaman came from aft where General Sherman had been corralled. "Hate to see you go," said the mate. "Between dominoes and poker, you paid my ship's bills. I may not see another payday like you for a long time."

"It was a humbling experience, haven't played dominoes for a long time, but I got some of it back at poker," remarked Owen.

General Sherman came down the gangway tentatively. He, like his owner, was unsure of his land legs. Owen's gear arrived on the shoulders of a shipmate. Saddle, rope, blanket, and a Henry rifle. They were all well used, and well maintained. Last came a bedroll and saddlebags.

The sailor said, "Hope you find a safe harbor. Write down those tales you told us. Put them in a magazine or book. So long."

After leading the General around the cranes off-loading cargo and crates being trundled up from below, Owen began saddling and tying down gear. General Sherman gave out a huff, and leaving a deposit of road apples, followed his boss out of the dock yards.

They both, horse and man, looked worn and scuffed, but their spirits began to perk up as they got on a road. Stopping at the gate, Owen asked the guard, "How far to Palo Alto and the Stanford Ranch?"

The guard, looking them over, replied, "You know you're on the wrong side of the Bay, don't you? Unless you can get a boat ride across, it's gonna be at least three days. I'd stay along the shore and see if I couldn't hitch a ride to Redwood City or Palo Alto. Those would be your closest ports."

"Thanks for the info," said Owen.

Stopping at the first stables they saw, Owen asked the boy to give General Sherman some oats and water while he went into the little café nearby.

While eating a bowl of soup and some sour dough bread, he asked the waitress, "Do you know a boat-owner nearby that would take a man and his horse across the bay?"

Thinking about it, she said, "You have a horse? That means a big enough boat to take you both across. There's a boat dock about a half mile from here. You may have to wait, but he's outfitted to take you."

After going back to pick up and pay for Sherman, the two moved on south along the shore. Closer to two miles than one-half mile, Owen looked at a sign. There it was, a large wooden sign, an arrow pointed toward the bay. "Passengers, animals, and freight—Ports of Redwood City, Palo Alto, Rengstorff Landing, and San Jose.

With two sighs, the duo headed down the path. Reaching the end of the road, Owen saw a shack, a short dock, and several boats tied up or pulled on shore. A sign proclaimed the management.

Jaime Silva, Owner. Captain Silva's Boat Works.
Passengers, Animals and Freight.
Small Boats & Rentals available.

A young man about Owen's age came out of the shack. "Help you, sir? Climb down and have a seat."

"Can you get us to the other side, hopefully today, or this evening?" asked Owen. "General Sherman and I need to get to near Palo Alto. I've heard there's a big ranch over there that might take me on."

"Well, I can take you, but the General would have to wait. The only boats outfitted to take horses won't be back till morning," said Silva.

"Damn! I'll have to find a place for us both to put up for the night," replied Owen.

"My names Jaime Silva. I've got an extra bunk in my shack, and a place for General Sherman around back. We also rent out horses and wagons. There is feed and water back there. You can pay for it by telling me your travels. You know, you don't look like any cowhand I've ever seen. A pea-coat and stocking cap. Where's the Stetson, boots, and vest?"

After bedding down General Sherman, Owen unrolled his bedroll on an empty bunk, moved into the kitchen, and sat down at a small table covered with oil cloth.

"What's your story?" asked Jaime. "You look a little frazzled. By the way, call me Jamie. This and fishing have been the family business for 40 years. My family came from the Azores to find gold. My grandfather discovered he could make more gold mining the miners, so he bought a couple of the abandoned boats. One to fish and one for transport. We have several boats on the coast near Pescadero. My father and brothers run those, which is good because I prefer this work."

Digging into a bowl of stew and home baked bread, Owen began his story. "My name's Owen William Pugh, from Wales. My family were miners, like moles in the ground. I didn't want that; heard they were picking up gold off the ground in 1880 in Colorado. I thought that's my kind of mining, so went to Cardiff and signed onto a ship for America. Landed in every port on the Atlantic Coast, ended up in New Orleans. Decided I'd seen enough ocean and got paid off."

"Okay, but from your gear and saddle, you worked cattle. How did that happen?" Jamie asked.

"Caught a cattle boat going back to Galveston. Started working as a do-every-chore hand on a ranch. Some of the vaqueros and Black cowboys took pity on me and taught me the ropes. In two years, I could ride, rope, brand and herd cattle. Some bad weather, but no waves, and all above ground."

"How did you get to the West Coast?" queried Jamie.

"Heard about California, wanted to see it, so I joined up with some migrants. None of us had the money to come by rail. They had a batch of patch-work wagons and buggies. Came west on the old trail to Los Angeles. I could drive a wagon and herd their few cattle, so they let me join them. It was hot, dry, and ugly. That town will never make it. Heard Nor-Cal was better, so signed on as a hand on a coastal trader. The clothes came out of the slop chest on board. Let me off on the wrong side of the Bay and here I am with General Sherman, a (name not popular in Texas,) and all my worldly goods," finished Owen.

"Well, we'd best get to bed. The boat will be here early, sun-up probably. See you in the morning, Jamie replied as he exited.

Murmuring to himself, Owen said, "I think this is my last stop. I think I'm home."

Owen woke early. The sun was barely up over the eastern hills. Hills, thought Owen, at least three are as high as Snowden. The rooster alarm went off again from behind the building, as he rolled out of bed, pulled on the dungarees, and donned his cleanest shirt.

"Morning," sounded a soft feminine voice from the kitchen area. "Jamie's checking out the boat,   setting it up for your horse. He's an old sweetie. I gave him a carrot and some apple slices, and he nuzzled my head while eating. I'm Teresa Marie, Jamie's cousin. There's coffee on the stove."

Owen took a longer look at her as she walked off. A small woman with a brisk walk. Her hair was a mix of caramel and light brown, twisted into loose braids coiled around the top of her head. A few stray tendrils showed a tendency to curl from the natural moisture in the air and the steam in the kitchen. His attention came back to the outer doorway as Jamie came rushing in.

"Sleep all right, Owen? Should have warned you about the rooster. He sets a tight schedule. Likes to give the first crow in the morning. He's a good sailor, too. Often joins us on short trips. Shows off his shiny, brassy cape to the seagulls and other roosters. A real show-off."

"Let me get my possessions and saddle, and I'll meet you at the boat," replied Owen.

"No need. We will load them on a cart and wheel them down. We're a true shipping business. We handle almost all situations," said Jamie.

Owen heard hoof beats from outside the door. I heard Teresa's voice from outside. When she appeared in the room, Owen gave her a surprised look. She was wearing a short heavy jacket, knit cap, rope soled sandals and her skirt was rolled up and pinned well above her ankles.

"You're going with us?" Owen said in a husky voice.

"Well, yes. I'm part of the family and the whole family works. I crew, work in the office, and cook in the little restaurant when needed. By the way, you didn't get breakfast. Here's an egg and ham sandwich. There's coffee in the cabin on the boat," and Teresa walked up the planks with General Sherman placidly following behind.

"Bye the way," Jamie said, "Teresa is more like a sister and daughter in our family. Her parents and brother died in a cholera epidemic, so my family raised her as one of us, uses the Silva name when she wants. Most people know us, and no one, no one, messes with her."

Owen took the subtle hint and looked her over more closely. She was slim, not skinny, not beautiful, but pretty. Her features were delicate, almond shaped eyes of hazel which turned green out of the sunlight, set off by large lashes. Maybe the eyebrows were too heavy. Then she smiled, pretty turned to beautiful, and Owen was smitten.

"I'll have to be careful around her and the family," he thought. "What the Americans call a straight arrow. Hell, I am an American."

"Hey, quit daydreaming and give us a hand with the sail. Show us you were really a sailor," called out Teresa.

"Yeah, sure. Anything for you!" replied Owen.

He quickly moved over to the ropes and spar, and showing off a little for Teresa' sake, did as he was told. The boat, almost flat-bottomed, sailed easily, slightly cross-current toward the west bay shore.

Owen, looking around and behind him at the disappearing shore and dock as the fog closed in, called to Jamie, "What are those white mounds behind us on the shoreline?"

Jamie spoke up, explaining, "Those are what's left of the local Indians' oyster harvests. There used to be a lot of native oysters in the bay. Between over-harvesting and fill-in, they're only found in some cleaner water areas. The bay tribes used to harvest them. Those shells are all that remains. A lot of them have been hauled away and either crushed for paving or baked and processed for the minerals. I guess that's progress."

"Have you seen any of the Missions—Monterey, San Gabriel in the south? Most of them up here have fallen apart and been carved up," asked Teresa. "That's where a lot of us went to school."

"We saw a couple in New Mexico and Arizona, but they were mainly ruins," replied Owen.

The shore was gradually becoming visible as the fog began to wisp away. With Teresa at the wheel, Jamie began to oar the boat into the channel leading to the harbor. Owen could see piers, ramps, and some smaller boats pulled up on the shoreline, which had been covered with gravel or the crushed oyster shells. Some smaller redwood logs also provided access through the bay mud and muck.

Jamie explained the situation: "We share the harbor with a couple of other companies, some fishermen, and private boat owners. Our family more or less manages it, but it's kind of a co-op."

As the tide was partly in, the boat came up about even with the dock. Jumping over the bow rail, the two men tied up while Teresa edged them into the pier. Jumping back on, the three of them brought in the sails, wrestling the plank gangway onto the boat. Jamie and Teresa checked out the ropes and lashing, while Owen pitched his meager gear on the dock.

Teresa brought General Sherman to the plank walkway. He hesitated, and as Owen was about to blindfold him, Teresa gave him a pat, a fresh biscuit, and a kiss. Without hesitation, he followed her onto the dock, and was rewarded with another biscuit, and stood calmly waiting for Owen.

"Hey, don't I at least get a biscuit? I didn't see those before. All I got was a sandwich," exclaimed Owen.

"Maybe, in the future, if you're as sweet as he is," remarked Teresa.

As the next few weeks went by, Owen found himself more and more frustrated. There were few ranch jobs available, a country-wide depression had settled in and eastern railroad monopolies controlled fees and stifled some of the commerce. Most of the ranch jobs were filled by California vaqueros whose families had been bound to the missions, and then to the rancheros, now in the hands of Yankees or Europeans. Owners were looking for managers and foremen with experience.

His salvation came from the Silva family. For room and board for himself and General Sherman, Owen became a sailor, deckhand, and helmsman for Silva Transport. With the railroads controlling most freighting, locals had turned to the water transport to get to the San Francisco, Sacramento, and smaller markets. It also allowed him to see Teresa frequently, as she spent more time in the office.

The General was getting fat. Too little action and too many treats from Teresa. Owen asked Teresa, "Can you ride? I mean western style, astride, not side-saddle."

"Sure," she replied, "I bet every girl in California can ride, especially if they live in the country. How do you think we got to school?"

"I don't know. It's different all over this country. In Wales my sisters and other girls seldom got to go to school beyond 14 or 15. If they were lucky, they got work as maids or as shop girls. Some even went into the mines, sorting coal and ore. It was a tough life for women," remarked Owen.

"Teresa, do you have a horse you can ride? I'd let you ride General Sherman, but he's not used to skirts and might be shy, and that working saddle is too big for you."

"Oh, I've got a saddle and a mare in the pasture that I ride, but don't worry about me and the General. I've been on his back whenever you're away. He likes to herd the cows and sheep, even the ducks and chickens. We're old companions," explained Teresa.

"Well, be careful. He is trained to be a cutting horse and he might take a notion to single out a cow or goose and take off," cautioned Owen.

"Let's meet behind the corral after church on Sunday. I'll bring something to eat, there are some springs up in the hills where we can stop and eat," said Teresa.

"Will your family worry, be upset, if you go riding alone with me?" queried Owen.

"Oh, no. They know you by now, and my brothers vouch for you. Besides, I trust you. And there's the fact that my brothers would beat the hell out of you, if I were harmed," Teresa said laughingly.

Late Sunday morning Owen saddled up the General and waited for Teresa. She came from the house. Owen's eyes widened as he saw her: hair in a bun, saucy hat on her head, drawstring under her chin.

A split riding skirt with half boots peeking out and a glimpse of pants cut off just above stockings. Owen looked at his reflection in a window. New hat to replace the worn cap, clean but worn double buttoned tan shirt, worsted wool trousers, worn but freshly polished boots. What in the world does this woman see in me? he thought.

"Can you rope Ramona and lead her to the fence for me? I'll climb the rails and get on from there. She's not used to skirts any more than the General."

Owen took his lariat off the saddle, one quick flick and it landed over the mare's nose. He noticed that she came docilely over to the fence and thought, "I could have just whistled her over." He took the waiting saddle off the rail and placed it and the horse blanket on her back, cinched it tight, and led her to Teresa.

"Well, you really are a cowboy. That was as neat as any of the local boys."

Seating herself, Teresa moved through the gate Owen held open. "Catch me if you can," she called out laughingly and took off at a canter.

Owen watched her move toward the hills. "I hope so," he thought.

Moving onto the saddle, he gave the General a nudge with his knee and moved after Teresa. She was a good horse woman. He reminded himself that she had been riding for a lot longer than he had. He had started with old, often broken-down horses.

He'd been terrified when the men put him on a new horse. It looked wild, eyed him a challenge as it waited. Owen didn't know what to expect. He'd seen others get a rough ride. He mounted quickly, the pony gave a few introductory mild bumps, turned his head, rolled his eye at Owen, as if to say, "What did you expect?" This remained his main horse as he learned the ropes of cowboy-ing.

Observing horses at work, their attitudes, faults and often mistreatment, Owen saved up his money to buy his own horse. General Sherman came up for sale when his owner broke a leg and was laid up for several weeks. The General was not flashy—bronze brown with a white blaze on his forehead. He looked slow and somewhat lazy when he worked, but Owen noticed it was more a deliberate and calculated move. Talking to the man that sold him, he was told, "The horse knows more than I do. He knows where the steer's going to go, it seems. He makes it look easy and made me look better than I really was. He is a gentleman. Responds to voice, knee, or rein signals. I wouldn't sell him, but I may never cowboy again."

Owen asked, "Why did you sell him to me? I know you had better offers."

"I've watched you. You have a way with your mounts and other animals. You never beat or kick your mounts and other animals. You never beat or kick your horse, nor a cat, nor dog.

General Sherman may look old but check his teeth. He's only about five or six. You're going to be his partner, not just his owner."

Teresa led them to a group of large oak trees. A small stream slipped through the rocks, gathered in rivulets and formed a small pond, before sedately joining the larger creek heading toward the bay.

Dismounting, then helping Teresa out of the saddle, Owen looked at her and the surrounding landscape. "Now I've seen the two most beautiful things in my life," he said.

"What's that?" Teresa asked.

"You and the land." Owen replied.

"Oh, you've been on the boats too long. You'll see other things and people more appealing," Teresa said, avoiding his glance and his smile.

"Oh, I've seen pretty places in Wales, green and wild, and calm seas near beaches and rocky shores, but not this combination," remarked Owen.

"I heard you talking one time to Jamie," Teresa said, attempting to divert the conversation, "but why did you leave Wales? Your whole family lives there. I know you didn't want to be in the mines, but was it so bad that you chose to leave family and friends? Did you have family here, know where you were going?"

Owen, looking pensive, sat quietly thinking. Teresa didn't interrupt.

"Wales was controlled, dominated by mostly English land and mine owners. There were a few old Welsh families too, I'll admit, but they were intermarried or economically involved with the Brits. Most miners did okay, hard work, seldom saw the sun six days a week. When the price of coal, tin, or copper was high they did all right. But your homes were often owned by the company, the stores were mostly company owned. They could hire and fire at their whim, cut wages any time

"My grandfather had a farm, raised sheep and grain. When the coal vein went under his land, the mining company followed it, just like the gold mines in California and other states. The water was poisoned, smoke messed up the air, the sheep couldn't survive on the land that was left. My dad and two uncles went down in the mines, my unmarried aunts worked in the mills, and then emigrated to Canada and Australia after they married."

Teresa asked, "Why didn't you go to Canada or Australia where you had relatives? It would have been easier. We didn't all come from Portugal in a group. Our families came over in small groups. They sent back for family. Even wives and children often came later. I know it looks like all family and neighbors, but Jamie and I, our cousins, were all born here. Now there are third generations. We seem clannish, but there are many intermarriages with other groups. We younger people consider ourselves 'Americans.' Only a few older persons talk about going back to Portugal."

"I will never go back to live there! I'm not a rebel, but one of the reasons I didn't go to Canada or Australia is that they're still British. No matter how hard you work, it's still hard to move up. You might become rich, but it will take three generations before your ancestry and class are not questioned. I had choices: the mine, the army, the shipyards. I chose to try it in the United States, win or lose on my own. I'm only 25, and someday I'll have land or a business of my own, I swear it."

"Don't you miss your family?" asked Teresa. "Do you write to them? I know you read and write as well as I do."

"It's slow, but I send letters, and sometimes I get letters back."

"I know, remember I handle all the local mail at the office," replied Teresa. "I see all the stamps and addresses. They come from all over the world."

"Well, my parents may never leave Wales. It's their home and all they know, but two of my brothers and my little sister will be immigrating legally as soon as we can pay off debt and buy tickets. If they land in New York or Philadelphia, they can come to San Francisco, even San Jose by train. If we do all right, we might even get our parents over. It's been ten years since I left, but I did send them a picture of me as a cowboy.

"We had better get back, your folks will be worrying. It's been a wonderful day. When we ride out next Sunday, we can switch horses and General Sherman can show you what he can do," remarked Owen.

"I hope it's every Sunday," replied Owen.

A month went by before Owen and Teresa went riding again. Owen had spent part of the time working on a boat going to Red Bluff. Only in the spring could you still get a boat that far up the Sacramento, and then only a flat or shallow hulled craft with an engine, navigating around mud flats and shallow sections. Jamie said that before long, Stockton would be the farthest they could go, regardless of rain and snow. Too much water was being diverted and dams were going up on the tributaries like the Feather, Yuba, and small streams. The Central Valley was a revelation to Owen.

He realized what Jamie was saying: Between the railroads and the navigation problems, the Silva freight business would have to change or die out. When they returned to the South Bay the extended Silva family met to discuss the situation. Owen sat in but didn't feel he had the knowledge or right to take part.

He had been in the South Bay almost a year. Seen the hills turn brown and a glorious green again,   reminding him of Wales. It seldom got cold enough to force him indoors, although the rains on the coast and in the mountains on the western side were heavy. That also reminded him of Wales.

"Do you ever get homesick?" asked Teresa. "The older people sometime talk about Portugal, how they miss some things, the village celebrations, customs. We have some of them here, you've gone to them with the family. Do you miss those things?"

"Oh, sure, but it was a pretty dull life mostly. Except for a few jobs, you work 10- or 12-hour days. You see the sunrise and sunset, maybe the only daylight you see is on Sunday, and the church wants you to spend the best hours within its walls. Too many of the men get drunk. Although there are the town football teams."

"Is it so different, what would you have done, were there no opportunities there?"

"I could have taken exams and maybe gone to university, but I would have ended up a clerk in an office or the church."

"Was there nothing else?" She asked.

"Well, I could have joined the army. The British have armies all over the world fighting in their colonies. I could have joined the American army too, if I felt like it. There are lots of Europeans in the U.S. Army. It's a hard life in either army, but if you're without a job, don't have opportunities, you get a bunk, food, and sometimes adventure. I didn't want to fight the Zulus in Africa, or the tribes in the Middle East, so why would I want to fight the Sioux or Apaches? When we traveled through New Mexico and Arizona, all we saw were people living in villages, farming, weaving, and herding animals. Custer and his troopers were dead by the 1880s; the only resistance was the Apaches. Even Quanah Parker was on a reservation in Oklahoma, whoever he is," answered Owen.

"Enough of this. Let's go riding. There are some places I haven't shown you. Have you seen the redwoods? Bay trees, the yellow slugs? You get General Sherman and Ramona saddled, while I change. I'll meet you at the stables."

Teresa led them out past the small spring. The meadow was still green, but the stream leading from the pool was now small and barely made a sound as it oozed more than trickled towards the now shallow creek. She took them upslope past enormous stumps of ancient redwoods, some big enough for dance floors.

Owen spoke out, "You could build a cabin on that and still have a solid wood floor. Where did they all go?"

Teresa explained that San Francisco had burned several times. "Every time it burned down, they just cut more trees and rebuilt. Some of the really old ones became foundations. It hardly ever rots and even lives through fires sometimes."

They moved into a grove of mostly old trees, some Owen thought well over 100 feet tall, maybe 200 feet. Taller than any ship's masts he had seen, and not feet, but yards, around.

"Close your eyes after you get off General Sherman," said Teresa. "I want to show you a special sight. Take my hand and don't look until I tell you to," leading Owen several yards into the cool of the forest, noiseless because of the mat of redwood leaves except for the call of jaybirds and the skittering of squirrels on the bark. "Okay, open your eyes."

It was dark enough that even having been closed, Owen's eyes had to adjust. "Tell me what you see," said Teresa, "Isn't it wonderful, a miracle?"

Owen was astonished. He was looking at a tree alive and well, a door sized opening into a burned hollow in the trunk with another opening on the other side, maybe even larger. "How does this happen? It's bigger than most cabins on ocean vessels. Why hasn't it died?"

"Someone told us the life is between the bark and the center wood. As long as most of the surrounding bark isn't burned, they continue to live," replied Teresa.

"You could live in here," remarked Owen.

"Some people have, from Indians to the present. I'm sure there are others like this one, someone else probably knows of it—Jamie and I discovered it as children, and only our closest friends have seen it."

"Does this mean I'm a close friend?" asked Owen breathlessly.

"You're more than a friend. I think of you as my beau," said Teresa as she moved into his embrace.

Owen pulled her into his arms and kissed her and kept her captured. She didn't resist. This time she kissed first, and then they both needed to breathe. They moved away from each other, still in the embrace. Owen aware that his arousal was very likely apparent to both of them, gave Teresa a hug and kiss and huskily said, "I'll go get the horses. We need to talk."

"I'll be right here," replied Teresa, sitting down abruptly on a nearby stump, a blush on her cheeks, her eyes wide, a slight smile on her face.

Owen, talking to General Sherman and Ramona "You know it's what I hoped and wished for, you've been witnesses. I love her, but how can I support her? I need a job with a future. I'm working all the time, but if it wasn't for the Silvas, I'd have to scrounge work." Leading the horses into the tree shadows, Owen saw that Teresa had reassembled herself, hair tucked back into the small, brimmed hat, a smile on her face, thoroughly composed. I wonder if I look that way, Owen thought, or only foolish.

Teresa looked up at Owen. "Where do we go from here, Owen? I love you, but what do you feel?"

Owen sat down beside her on the stump. "Teresa, it should be obvious how I feel. I've adored you since that first time I saw you in the kitchen. Then you were the pert sailor girl on the boat. Old Sherman took to you immediately, and he's a good judge of people. Adoration turned to love. You're sweet, kind, resourceful, and beautiful in looks and spirit. How could I not love you? Will you marry me, please?"

"Of course I'll marry you, but you will have to get permission from my father. That's a formality and tradition. The whole family likes you, and Jamie is always talking you up. He respects you and thinks of you as family."

"Well, Teresa Marie Silva, will you marry me, after I ask your father, in front of your family, for your hand?"

"Owen, my last name isn't officially Silva, but he is my father, the only family I have ever known."

"Let's clear this up. What name should go on the wedding certificate, Miss Teresa Marie? My family will want to know if I'm marrying a slag-heap or a shop-girl. We have our pride, you know. When we come out of our holes, we want the best."

"You silly goose, of course I have a last name. You can tell your family you're marrying Teresa Marie Rose, whose mother's name was Sylvia Elizabeth Dutra, and father's name was Arturo Romero Rose."

"Let's get back home before it gets dark. I have to talk to your father," Owen said as he lifted Teresa to her saddle.

"Oh, don't worry, the family is aware of my intentions towards you. My sisters and cousins have been counting the days until you committed yourself."

"Was I that obvious?" asked Owen.

"Even Jamie wondered what was holding you back," replied Teresa. "He said you were always asking him about other men, who was I seeing, did I go to dances when you weren't here, who came around the office or store most often."

"Teresa, you know I have very little job prospects. If it weren't for your family, I would be always looking for work. You can't support a wife on a cowboy's wages, and your father and Jamie have enough family to really handle the fishing boats and freight. Now that the railroad runs down to San Jose and southern California, that is going to slow down."

"Oh, Owen, don't worry so much. It will work out. You're a hard worker, a quick learner. Things will be better. The family is shifting into other fields. Papa says we're land rich and money poor, but more people are coming every day. "

The sun was still up when they reached the Silva home and since it was Sunday, most of the family was there. Owen had picked up some Portuguese, but the questions and answers were coming so fast and overlapping, that he was unable to sort it out. The sisters and younger women swooped down on Teresa as many of them called her and swept her off. Owen was left holding the horses until some of the younger boys took them away, climbing onto Sherman's and Ramona's backs as they moved to the barn. Owen was amazed at General Sherman's tolerance, then realized that Sherman spent more time there than he did.

Esteban Silva stepped out of the house. "Owen, my daughter tells me you need to speak to me about some personal affairs. Why don't you come into the kitchen? Hermalinda, Teresa's mother will meet us there. A cup of coffee, Owen? Maybe some lemonade, from our own tree."

"Owen, relax," said Hermalinda coming in with a pitcher of lemonade with ice chunks clinking in it. "We've been expecting this, even if you haven't."

Owen's hands felt clammy even before he took up the cold, sweating glass. Mr. Silva, Mrs. Silva, I have admired and loved your daughter, Teresa Marie for a long time. Now it has come to my attention that she also loves me. I know my prospects aren't good, right now, but I will do my very best to make her and keep her happy. Please allow me to make her my wife."

"Owen, the whole family has been aware of your feelings for some time. We've been watching you and getting reactions from friends and the people you've dealt with for us and on your own. Everyone likes you—they say you're honest, do your share, and more. Even more, they say, you're willing to ask for and accept advice. You're a good man, with ambition."

Hermalinda spoke up, "More importantly, our daughter loves and respects you. You've never taken advantage of her or betrayed her trust. That's rare in these days."

Together they responded, "We welcome you into our family, Owen Pugh."

A loud cheer and laughter, tittering, and giggles came from the other room. A concertina, fiddles, a guitar, and ukulele brought back from Hawaii began playing some Stephan Foster and popular songs. Hermalinda and a married daughter stepped into the room and it hushed. She began to sing Portuguese cantos in a soft alto voice, her daughter joining her in a plaintive love song. Owen understood little of the words but caught the meaning and spirit. Someone uncovered the organ and added it to the fiddles, now tuned as violins, and the guitar. When the song died out, someone began a wild, fast tempoed folk dance or reel. Owen thought, "I'm back in Wales or Cornwall." Glasses of wine appeared, the rug was rolled up, and the dancing began. A hand drum, stomping feet, picked up the tempo.

After watching a while, he picked up the movements. A soft hand slipped into his, and a voice near his ear said, "Dance with me, Owen" as Teresa slipped in front of him. More glasses of wine appeared, and the house began to tremble. Small children were swept up and danced around with parents, aunts, and uncles. Glassware nick-nacks disappeared and were transported to safety. All was well in the Silva household.

Owen and Teresa drifted outside when they got the chance. "Teresa, I have a couple of trips for the company coming up, I can't skip them. What should I do?" asked Owen.

"Don't worry about it. Between work and organizing the wedding, I'll be all tied up anyway. I would hardly see you. Then there is the dress and everything. Go do your work and when you come back, we can decide on a date, a place, wedding attendants. I know that's not a problem for you, but I'm going to have to pick and choose. Then I will have to placate and find jobs for the others."

Jobs and family kept Owen and Teresa apart for ten days. Except for seeing each other at dinner when Owen was home, they had been separated. Even the Sunday rides had been accompanied by several nieces and nephews wanting to be outside before the weather changed. General Sherman and Ramona spent much of the time cutting off and herding back wandering children. Except for a few older ones, most didn't know they were being safeguarded by the two patient guardians, allowing Owen and Teresa to talk and plan.

"Terrie, I don't have an engagement or wedding ring," Owen said, "I want you to have a ring to show everyone. Is there a reliable jeweler around here? I do have some small Mexican gold coins from Texas. They could be melted or traded for a ring."

"Let's ask Jamie, he knows everybody that crosses the bay in small boats. He says he meets people in every trade. Some are pretty secretive and cautious, especially if transporting something valuable like jewelry or loose gems. I wager he knows a jeweler or his associate."

Two weeks went by before Owen, Teri, with Jamie and his girlfriend, Soledad Brannon, pulled their buggy up to the stables at the train station in Mayfield. None of them had been on a train, and the idea of taking the fairly new SFSJ railroad to San Francisco was an adventure. Also, it let them off almost downtown where the jewelers were. Leaving the horse and buggy to the stable boy, they walked to the depot. Taking their tickets, the two men helped the ladies into the car.

"Owen, this is pretty nice. We can all face each other and talk. Can I have the window seat?" Terrie asked.

Soledad took the other window seat. "Jamie says the train goes really fast between towns. I've never gone faster than a canter. Can we open a window?" she inquired.

Jamie, the only one to have ridden a train, said, "Well, maybe in the slow sections. Sometimes the coal smoke blows back and it's nasty. Occasional cinders, too. Let's just see how it goes. It's faster than any ship, that's for sure."

"How safe is it? Steam is pretty powerful. I remember seeing wrecked steamboats on the Mississippi and news stories about engines blowing up. They used them in the mines to raise and lower lifts and pump out water," remarked Owen.

The train began to move with a rumble of metal rods and pistons, the chuffing of the steam powered engine raising the noise level to where speech was inaudible. Jamie stood and lowered the car's window as other passengers hastily did the same. Jamie spoke loudly, "It will get better as we move out. You know how loud the engines are on our boats—even the small ones are pretty noisy."

"What makes that clacking sound, it's so rhythmic?" asked Terrie.

"I'm not sure. It may be the engine parts working." replied Jamie.

"I know, I know," said Soledad excitedly, glad to be able to take part in the discussion. "My dad worked on the construction gangs and later in the ;train yards. He said where the iron rails join, there's a little gap. Not much, but a little one, and as the iron wheels go over them, they flex and move as it uses a clacking sound. He said that experienced engineers and other train workers can tell by the sound if there's a problem. They remember the section and the company can send a crew out to fix it."

The young women talked about the wedding, while staring out the windows as open space and buildings sped by, mesmerized by the speed. Owen and Jamie discussed the future and possibilities for the Silva family freighting business.

Arriving in San Francisco, they elected to walk to Market Street after the rocking, swaying ride on the train.

'Let's look at the rings in Gleins and Shreves," said Terrie, "The ladies said they're the best."

"Oh, yes," said Soledad, "my cousins' rings came from there."

Jamie cautioned them. "Well, look but don't act too eager. My friend, Jacob Swartzberg says he can duplicate any of their settings and stones at half the cost."

Coming to the first jewelers, they stopped at the windows to look at rings, broaches, and pins. The girls gaped at the variety and the prices.

Jamie said, "Let's go in. The better stuff is always inside, Jacob says, the better to protect it." After browsing and exclaiming over some of the rings, a salesman came over and offered to move some trays onto the counter. When the women hesitated, he asked if they wanted their fingers sized. While this took place, the two men observed the women's favored styles. Moving into the next shop, they asked the ladies to remember their favorites.

Exiting, they got on a streetcar that took them to a less opulent area. No fancy windows, locked doors; many of the men had beards, black suits and coats, some with strange hats. Although Terrie and the men had seen travelers of this type before, Soledad was observing them with wide eyes while clutching her cross. "Are these Jews?" she whispered to Jamie. "Are we safe?" she asked apprehensively.

Jamie whisked her through a door into a small showroom. "Soledad, Teresa, Owen, I would like you to meet my good friend, Jacob Swartzberg." A tall, muscular man, side curls, a greying black beard, stepped from behind a high desk. Doffing a flat-brimmed, flat-crowned hat, he bowed slightly to the ladies, then clasped Jamie in a bear hug and extended his hand to Owen.

"So, these are your friends and family. I've been waiting to meet them for a long time. Come, come, upstairs where I and my family live. My wife has fixed a sweet treat from our old homeland."

The stairway opened into a living room decorated in stark contrast to the lower show room. Bright colors, brocaded cushions, velvet covered chairs, a settee of soft leather with a matching ottoman. A large window looked onto a flowery, but manicured back yard with a wrought iron table, topped by a slab of polished redwood burl.

"Oh, it's so beautiful, we don't have anything like this at home," exclaimed Teresa, "Our garden is more informal, and mama raises vegetables with the flowers."

Soledad burst out, "Look at the table. I didn't know redwood could look so pretty, and this room is gorgeous."

"Friends, my wife Delma. She is the creator of all this beauty. She brought some of Lebanon to our household. We may never go back, but she brought some of the good memories to life."

Delma, blushing replied, "Jakey, you do go on, but you know I miss the sunshine of home. It is more like Southern California. When we go there to visit relatives, it reminds me of the warm sea and beaches. Would you ladies and gentlemen like some coffee, a sweet cake? I forget my manners."

The men sat and talking of business and California's government.

"So, you came from Lebanon," asked Owen. "I'm not sure where that is. Is it part of Europe? If it were English territory, I'd have heard tales, usually battles, as a lot of my relatives were in the British army."

Jamie said, "A lot of my Portuguese ancestors, even my grandpa, sailed there to trade. He said it was beautiful and one of the few places where all nations were accepted, and trade was freely welcomed."

"It was a good place," said Jacob, "but it was becoming more difficult under the new ruler. We were pretty free, but the special taxes and bribery made it hard to make a living. Here's not perfect, but business is business and we're free. My son and daughter go to public school. We encourage them to fit in, so they follow religious rules to an extent, but don't stand out from the other students."

Joining the women, Jacob led them to another doorway. "This is our workshop. Aaron and Yusuff do most of the designing and crafting. There are some others, but they often work at home. We use the lost wax process for custom jewelry.

"Teresa, Soledad, sit here at the counter." Opening a large safe set behind a cabinet Jacob pulled out a tray of unset stones and colored drawings of settings with various single and mixed stones. "Pick them up, hold them to the light, see what excites your fancy."

Owen, watching closely, spoke up. "Pick what you like, don't think of cost. It can all be worked out."

"You, too, Soledad If you're really attracted to something, speak out."

"I know diamonds are traditional, Owen, but I really like this stone. What is it, Jacob?", asked Teresa.

"That's a white cream opal from Australia, but notice, here's a fire opal. The one you like has some of the fiery streaks in it also. It's a beautiful stone."

"Can we get it Owen? Is it very expensive, Jacob? I really love it."

"It can be done. Owen and I will deal with it," replied Jacob.

Soledad looked at the stones. "Jamie did you really mean it? Can I really get a ring?"

"Of course, I meant it! But there is one thing you'll have to promise."

"What is it?" Soledad asked.

"You have to promise to become Mrs. Jamie Silva! Soledad Brannon, will you marry me?" said Jamie, taking her hand.

"Really, you're not playing with me? Do you mean it?" yelped Soledad. "Terrie, we can have a double wedding."

Arriving back at Mayfield in the early dusk, the two couples were met by Jamie's brother Manuel with the buggy and three of the cowboys.

Manuel looked them over. "Well, you look cheerful. Let Gilbert drive the ladies home, I have some news. Mount up, and I will tell you on the way."

Jamie and Owen, looking anxious, asked "Okay, what's happened that you didn't want the ladies to hear?"

Manuel spoke quietly. "Some thieves, punks really, robbed the store and office. Threatened Dad and Jesús. They didn't get much money, filled a bag with food and went off."

"That's not too bad," said Jamie, "What else?"

"They took two saddle horses and some buggy horses on the way out," said Manuel. "Unfortunately, the two horses were Sherman and Ramona. Jorge followed, but they got into the canyons. He thinks he knows where they're headed. Gilbert, tell them what happened."

"Mr. Pugh, that big ole General Sherman got loose and come galloping back. He came right up to me, whickered, and wanted me to follow him. I was afraid to go on by myself, so I came on back to the stables. I think it's best if we take after them early in the morning. He's a bad one, Jamie. Calls himself 'Young Tiburcio. Claims to be kin to Vasquez, you know the outlaw they hung in San Jose a while back."

"Oh yeh!" replied Jamie. "A lot of Californios lost land and power after the gold rush and U.S. takeover. It's an excuse for some to run wild, rob people, and rustle stock. I bet there's half a dozen calling themselves Tiburcio and Joaquin claiming to rob Anglos and help poor Mexicans and Indios."

"They haven't helped anyone I know," mentioned Manual. "They seem to rob everyone equally. Most of the money must go to whiskey and saloon keepers. Maybe to people hiding them."

Owen changed into rough clothes at the stables. Talking to Jamie, they agreed Jamie should stay behind, calm down his parents and the ladies, telegraph the local sheriffs and police departments for information and help. "Tell them we will meet them where Bean Hollow Road hits the coast or maybe at Waddell Creek. The others can search around and find us if they find a trail or signs."

Teresa came running from the house. "Oh, Owen, be careful! I know you have seen danger before, but these are bad men. 'Mucho mal hombres,' as they say in town. Watch out, listen to the men. They've lived around here for generations. Please, please, don't be foolish."

"I just got you. I'm not gonna do something stupid," Owen answered. "I'll listen to Manuel and Jorge. They're not going to take us into danger."

"We should go, Mr. Owen," said Gilbert, leading General Sherman and two more horses up to the group. The sun will be coming up in the east soon. We need to be where I quit last night."

"Bring back my Ramona, Owen," called Terrie, as they rode off.

Both Gilbert and Sherman seemed to know where they were going, so Owen let them set the pace. As the sun's glow, but not the sun, peeked over the mountains, Gilbert pulled up. "Here's where I stopped. There's where Sherman pawed and scuffed the ground. See his tracks coming back from the others in the soft ground. He was moving pretty fast."

"Can you lead us on a straight line? Maybe we can see where they were going and cut across. Pick them up again," asked Owen.

Manual replied, "Jorge, Gilbert, and I have hunted mountain lions and stock through here. There is only one way to take horses through and down these mountains, boss."

Owen, a little taken aback by being called "boss," spoke quietly to Manuel, "Segundo, it's your play. Lead the way."

Following a tunnel-like trail through the brush, they moved slowly, occasionally stopping to listen for hoof beats or crackling brush. Stirring up a few deer and some upset pigs, they kept on the trail. Breaking through, they caught a glimpse of the coast and sometimes the surf, but nothing was moving that they could see.

"Is that Pescadero Creek to the south? That looks like the pier with the Silva boats down there." Owen said, then asked the men "Where's Waddell Creek?"

"A few miles north, if we go down to the beach, longer if we stick to the hills," said Jorge. I think we should go on down to the shore. The tide's out and we can travel faster, probably spot the other posse quicker."

They had only been on the beach a little way when they were spotted by five riders coming from the north. Both groups reined up, identifying themselves with waves and shouts, they moved closer. Only then did they see two other riders on the cliffside above them, with rifles trained toward their group. Raising their arms and waving their hats, they continued toward the others. The two men dropped down a   narrow trail and joined them as the other group closed in.

"Deputy Swedlund, San Mateo County. What have you found? We came up from Pacifica after a   telegram from Redwood City and haven't seen hide nor hair of Young Tiburcio or anyone else. We've probably passed their hidey-hole."

"Jim Harris from the ranch to the east. Didn't see them but saw some disturbed cattle and deer moving out of the oaks and brush a little north.

It's pretty brushy country, so we didn't investigate."

Four more riders joined up, coming down the Montaro Bluff. "That's Riley Downs and Chick Daniels from San Jose. That was quick," said Swedlund. "How did you get here so fast?"

Riley spoke as he slid off his horse. "These punks robbed a couple of stores in the South County two weeks ago. Pistol-whipped the clerk when he wasn't quick enough. Tried to hold up the Hollister-Gilroy stage, but it was full of ranchers coming from a meeting. When the gang saw the guns popping from the coach, they took off. We took a boxcar out of San Jose, stopped at San Carlos, and came over the trail to here."

Conferring together, the men came to a decision. Since Swedlund and Downs had official jurisdiction, they decided to lead two groups of six, while Deputy Daniels joined Owens group to represent the Law.

"We should go back north to where you saw the disturbance," said Downs. "Give us a few minutes to hopefully get above them. If we come in from four sides, we should have them trapped. Wait until at least two of our groups have signaled or called out. We don't want a gunfight, if possible."

An hour or so later, Owen's group broke the brush above a small, isolated meadow. Below them, they saw the remains of a fire, nearby a coffee pot, skillet, and dirty cups and plates. They couldn't see the gang, but the horses were corralled by a make-shift brush and rope fence.

On sensing Ramona, General Sherman whickered loudly. When Ramona responded, men popped out from under the brush with pistols and rifles.

A voice boomed out of the brush on the other side. "This is Deputy Swedlund. Throw down your guns."

"You heard him. This is Deputy Daniels. Lay down sus pistoles and raise los manos."

"Okay, señores. We're coming out," said a voice from a tangle of bushes. "Don't shoot, por favor." Two young but tough looking men, more boys than men, eased out of the tangle.

"Drop your guns and gun belts, if you've got one," called Deputy Swedlund.

Another voice from higher up the gulley yelled, "Los cabardos fight back. Shoot them!" Rifle bullets whizzed around Owen and his cowboys. Horses bucked and backed off. Again, Deputies called out as the other posses arrived.

"Is that you, Tiburcio? Give up! You're surrounded. You can't escape," called out the San Jose posse.

"That's what you think, gringo! Come and get me."

More pistol shots buzzed around them.

Owen felt his head explode and he sagged in the saddle. He heard Manuel and Jorge as they caught him, while Gilbert grabbed the reins and talked to General Sherman.

Manuel spoke quietly, "You're all right, boss. A bullet creased your head. You'll have a neat scar to show your kids. You can always comb your hair over it. Can you hear me?"

Owen spoke up and the buzzing in his head eased, but the pain got stronger. "Get me back up on the General. I think we can leave this to the others."

The other posse came into the clearing. "We got three of them, but Young Tiburcio and another got away. We got your horses back, though."

Five other riders came leading Ramona and the other horses. "Looks like they picked up a couple more horses and the pack mule from our ranch. The rest of the men are scouring the brush, but it looks like they either got into another hidey-hole or vamoosed somehow. We'll get 'em though."

Owen spoke a little unclearly, "Well, we got Terrie's Ramona back. That's good! Can you boys sneak me in? Just tell Terrie I'm worn out and will see her tomorrow. She'll just fret and yell at me, if she sees me like this.

Checking the kitchen to see if it was clear, the men helped a slumping Owen into the room, down a corridor and into a small bedroom. Easing him on to a large cot, Owen spoke softly, "See if you can get Jamie in here without Terrie's knowing what happened." As he finished, Jamie popped into the room and shut the door behind him.

"Okay, what happened? How bad is it? Let me see. Manuel, get Dr. Sloan. He's a vet, but he knows about wounds."

Hermalinda came in quietly saying, "You men think you're so sly. One of the servant girls saw you and got it out of her husband. How bad's the wound? Let me see. Oh-ee, not so bad, but an inch or two over, and I'd be laying you out and calming Teresa. Jamie, bring me the bottle of carbolic, soap, water, and one of the old pillowcases. Maybe some laudanum in the medicine chest. Jorge, you know the spikey aloe plants outside the kitchen—bring me two of the big leaves.

"Well, Owen, you're going to have a scar, but your hair will cover it." She went to work as the items arrived. As she trimmed the hair around the wound, Owen winced, but gave a muffled ouch as she washed the wound with diluted carbolic acid. Coating the crease with a thick layer of aloe, she covered the spot with a pad, and wrapped it with strips ripped from the pillowcase.

"There, that will do for now. We don't need the doctor. You may have a concussion, so one of us will be in and wake you, if you can sleep. If the pain gets too bad, we can give you some laudanum, but try to get by without it. Teresa and Solé are showing off their rings and talking double wedding. I'll try and keep them going and let Teresa think you're worn out. Oh! She's really happy about her horse and spent some time with Ramona and Sherman. Good night."

Owen spent a painful and restless night. It seemed like every time he dozed off, Jamie or Esteban came to check on him and quiz him. Later he found out that the doctor, a civil war veteran, had told them what to watch for and what to ask. He woke the next morning with the opening of the curtains to bright sunlight, a headache, and the glaring eyes and stern frown of Teresa.

"What were you thinking, did you really think you could keep a secret from me? All the ladies whispering, giving me rueful smiles, their men slinking around corners, talking outside the barn. When I went out to see if Ramona was all right, the men stopped talking. I knew something wasn't right. I saw mama dump a pan of bloody water, I looked in the trash bin and saw your bandana with dried blood stains. I cornered Gilbert in the stables and coaxed it out of him."

"Terrie honey, it's not that bad. It was a wild shot. I just happened to be in the wrong place. It is just a crease. Ask your mother," said Owen.

"You got my own mama, papa, and brother covering for you. You should be ashamed, and after you promised me you would stay out of danger," she said, then broke into tears.

Owen sat up quickly, wincing at the pain, "Don't cry, honey, I'm all right. Why I could get up right now."

"No, you won't," cried Teresa, 'You'll stay right there until mama or the doctor says you can get dressed, and I will be right here to make you follow their orders."

Another night and day went by with Teresa nursing and fussing over him. When she left for a time, he sneaked up and paced the room, getting back into bed when he heard her footsteps. When night came, he was still awake after supper. The sound of Teresa' footsteps came down the hall and the door opened.

"Going to read me some Dickens. That Kip is a lot like me, great expectations."

"No, nothing that easy. I've got a remedy that I think will perk you up," she said, sliding into the   narrow cot with him. "Why you must be running a fever, you're so hot." She stepped out of the covers and casually dropped her nightgown to the floor. "I need to get you out of those long johns, before you swoon Oh, my!

They seem to be stuck on something Excuse me, I need to clear something."

"Terrie, are you sure? You remember the promises we made," Owen said in a strangled voice.

"Shut up, Owen. I talked with mama and my aunts, and they said it was okay. Forget the church. We're practically married anyway. I want you to know what you would have missed if you had gotten killed."

The bedding was on the floor: they both realized that she had gotten his attention.

After a few moments, Owen whispered, "Terrie, I can't hold much longer, are you sure?"

"Yes, Owen," she breathed huskily. They both shuddered simultaneously After a few minutes regaining their breaths, Owen flipped her on her back and entered her again. This time it was longer and gentler. He broke off first, looked at her flushed face, and said, "I truly, truly love you, you know."

"Yes, Owen, I'm sure of it. I always have been."

Unable to sleep after Terrie had left, Owen arose and got dressed. Looking in the mirror, he examined the wound on his head. It was already healing, but he couldn't put his hat over the bandage or leave it exposed to the curious. Looking in his duffle-bag he came up with a soft cap, a remnant of his Welsh days. He hadn't seen General Sherman since he'd been hustled into the room, so he wandered out to the stables as the sun was coming up.

Whickering, snorting, and grunting, General stuck his head over the half-door to greet him. Owen gave him a pat and a hug, while General Sherman reached for the apple slices Owen held out. Munching on the slices, General Sherman followed Owen into the coral. Owen spoke to his horse in a soft voice, "Well, boy, we had quite an adventure, didn't we? You were a big help finding Terrie's horse, but if you could have kept quiet a little longer, maybe I wouldn't have been shot." General Sherman rolled his eyes and reached for another apple slice, then nudged Owen with his head as if to say, I know, but it's all over now.

Entering the kitchen, the cook handed him a cup of coffee and a knowing smile. Jimmy, another brother, and Terrie's father sat down, and plates of sausage, eggs, and potatoes appeared. The younger men gave him a searching look and Terrie's father spoke up.

"How are the wedding plans going? Have the four of you set a date? Maybe you should make it sooner rather than later."

Her mother came in from the hall, saving Owen from a reply. "Teresa will be down later. She said she was tired after all the hours nursing. Said she thought Owen was almost healed." She and the cook giggled and turned toward the stove. Owen blushed, while Papa Silva gave him a scowl that turned into a small smile. "Must be time for you to be up and busy, if Teresa has cleared you."

After checking on some stock, Owen met with Manuel and Gilbert to discuss any ranch problems. The topic of the posse came up when Owen removed the cap and the men saw the scar peeking from the bandage.

Gilbert remarked, "Ayee, that was pretty close, boss. Looks like it's healing pretty well, thank God."

Manuel looked it over. "It will give you good, bold stories to tell. How you fought off the dreaded outlaw, Tiburcio. You don't have to say which one. If you had gotten yourself killed, we would have had to leave the ranch. Miss Teresa would never have forgiven us. She can have a sharp tongue when she's displeased, which, thank goodness, isn't very often. Her last treatment seems to have worked well." He grinned and laughed out loud as he cantered off with Gilbert and Jorge toward the cattle.

Trotting back to the ranch, Owen held up as Terrie came riding towards him on Ramona. Sliding from the saddle, he helped her down, giving her a hug and kiss as she came into his arms.

"What are you doing up and working? Are you sure you're all right? Take off that silly cap and let me look at the wound. Well, that looks pretty good," said Terrie.

Stuffing his soft cap into his jacket pocket, he pulled Terrie close and kissed her. Taking the horses' reins in his free hand, the pair began walking back toward the stables. As Owen released the horses, unsaddled and loosed them into the corral, he turned to Terrie, saying, "You know, I feel a little weak. I think I may be having a setback. Do you think you can give me another treatment tonight?"

"Well maybe, but those treatments take a lot out of the nurse, too. Don't count on it. It's an old family remedy used on special occasions," said Terrie as she flounced off into the house.

"Owen, got two letters for you at the office. One's from Britain about six weeks old, the other's from Philadelphia, about a week old. They came a day apart. One of the clerks asked if you would let him have the stamp from Britain for his collection?" Jamie asked.

Neatly opening the letter to save the stamp, Owen handed the cover to Jamie. "It's from my brother, Dayfid (David). He and my younger sister are coming to the U.S." Skimming, then rereading more carefully, he looked at Terrie and Jamie.

"Well, what's it say?" asked Terrie, excitedly "When will they get here? When was it mailed? Tell us, when will they get here?"

"Dayfid mailed it the day before they were to sail from Liverpool. They could already be here! In the states at least. Everyone's well, doing okay in England. My sister Bronwyn's healthy. He says they're bringing me a surprise."

"Well, open the other letter, duffus. It may have more information if it was mailed from the East,"Terrie said.

Ripping the letter open and again skimming it first, Owen yelped. "They landed in Philadelphia. They must have beaten the packet ship, or it got held up somewhere. They are trying to get tickets on a train for San Jose, that was last week. They could be here now, if they don't get delayed."

"That means they will be here for the wedding. You will have family here. Your sister will have to be a bridesmaid. Oh, how exciting! I need to tell mama and papa."

Owen, speaking to himself out loud, said, "Where will I put them? Can I support them? They can't have much money left."

Jamie, overhearing, spoke up quickly. "They are family, Owen, we will find a way. There is plenty of room, and Terrie's family has space, If they are like you, there won't be a problem.

On the trip back to San Jose, the two men had talked about the future. Would the freight business hold up? Would the railroads drive them out of   business? Would the towns on the peninsula keep growing? They were worried

255

about the survival of the Silva businesses, should they expand or cut back? Jamie thought the bulk freighting and passenger business would be okay for several more years, but the family would have to be alert and change with the times. The fishing fleet would have to cooperate with the San Francisco fisheries or lose the larger market.

Owen brought up the cattle and sheep ranches. They agreed there would be a growing market for meat as the towns were filling up the open spaces and the population growing. The people might still have chickens, but cows take more space and attention. They agreed to talk things over with Jamie's family.

Two hours later they pulled into the station to find a buggy waiting. A couple hours later, they arrived at the Silva house.

The family came boiling out to meet them. Terrie and Soledad hugging and kissing them as if they had been gone for a month instead of two days.

"Owen, close your eyes, we've got a surprise for you." Leading him into the kitchen and sitting him down, Terrie said, "Keep them closed. Don't peek." Owen heard footsteps and a rustle of skirts.

"Now you can open them."

His older brother David, stood before him, and peering out from behind him was a young woman. It couldn't be his sister—she was a little girl.

"Well, Owen, aren't you going to welcome your family?" said Terrie.

Shaking hands and then hugging his brother, Owen, breaking down, said, "David, when did you get here?" Where's Bronwyn? Who's this young lady?"

"Oh, Owen, don't you recognize your little sister?" the girl asked.

"But you're a young lady—my sister's a little girl," stammered Owen. "I don't believe it; you look like Momma from the wedding picture. David when did you get here? Why wasn't I told when you would arrive?"

"You can talk about that later, Owen. We have another surprise for you," said Terrie. "Close your eyes again." Owen heard movement and some giggles.

"Open your eyes, Owen, here's your big surprise."

Opening his eyes, Owen looked around. Someone new had entered the room.

"Hello, darling, how's my brave boy?" said a familiar voice.

Looking around to the doorway, Owen spoke excitedly "Momma, Momma! You're here? In California! I thought I'd never see you again."

"It's amazing! Now I've got some of my own family in America. Truthfully, I thought I might never see any of you again. Bronwyn, you're a young woman. In my mind, you are still a young girl. Momma, your hair's a little grayer, but you look much the same as when I left you crying in the doorway. Davy, you're way bigger than I remember and with a beard, you look like a proper English gent. What about the rest of the family?"

"Owen, you've become a man," sniffed his mother. Where is my young son? You look tan and weathered, no miner's slump for my boys."

"Davy, what about the rest of the family, what are they doing? Except for the letter announcing when you left and when you were arriving, there wasn't much family news."

All three started answering at the same time.

"Wait, wait, one at a time!" cried Owen. Davy spoke up before his sister and mother could intervene. "Wesley's apprenticed and worked with a company geologist and engineer. He is going to Canada to work at a company mine. Is that a long way from here? The train trip from Omaha was a long one. Is all of this land so big? I thought we might be close to him"

"Brother, Canada is bigger than the States. I'll show you some maps next week. What about Maureen?"

"You know she married the younger son of a mine owner."

"Yes, Harold Bixby, seemed all right for a mine owner's son, good soccer player," recalled Owen.

"Well, his older brother passed on, flu or TB or something. Harold's now the heir to the mining company. Maureen's on the way to being Lady Bixby," explained Davy.

"Good God! Welsh society will never recover. We will have to watch ourselves, if we see her again," said Owen.

"Oh, we will. As soon as he takes over, they are going to make a Grand Tour. We're on the list. Especially now that her family is here.

"Momma, I thought you would never leave home. What changed your mind?"

"Well, when your father passed, I looked around and I said, Mary Elizabeth, there is nothing to hold you here. If your family is all leaving, you don't want to grow old alone. Oh, some of your dad's old gents came round, but I said to myself I've been a miner's wife once and that's enough. I sold the house back to the company.

Bronwyn and I opened a millinery and sewing section in Rupert the tailor's shop, and between the three of us and Maureen's help, we got tickets to America, not steerage, mind you, but an actual cabin. It was small, but okay, and we could get on deck. Didn't even get sea sick, and here I am in California, where all the names are funny. Why, they're almost as bad as Welsh."

Owen kept active with secretive trips around the San Francisco Peninsula and South Bay, sometimes gone for two or three nights. Terrie stayed busy with the wedding and work in the shipping office. She seldom got on a boat anymore and missed it.

The Pugh family also took up her time. Getting acquainted with Owen's mother, Mary, and sister, Bronwyn, an unusual name to Terrie, took up more time. The two future mothers-in-laws were about the same age and delighted each other in their differences. Owen's mother, Mary was British in speech and customs, while Hermalinda was American born, with a mix of Portuguese and American customs.

"Tell us about Owen," urged Hermalinda, "except with Teresa he's pretty quiet. He doesn't open up to anyone but her and Jamie. We don't even know much about his life after he came to the U.S., even his time in Texas. We know he became a cowboy when he came to California on the old Southern trail but that's about all."

"My Owen was always the adventurous one. All my children were smart and ambitious. No going down the mines for them, at least not for long. They saw what it did to their father and uncles, and the families. They have all tried to better their lot and they have, but Owen's the only one that took off so early. Young, he was 15 when he left. We got a letter when he turned 16 in the U.S. He was a boy when he left. Now, when I see him, he's a man. I only recognized him because he looks like all the Pugh men. It's a good thing he found Teresa, she'll keep him steady. From his letters, I feel like I already know her, and her family. Why, you have been as much of a family as his own. I thank you for that," finished Mary.

"Call me Linda, no one knows my whole name in the family," said Teresa's mother. "Teresa had her eyes on him after the first few meetings. The way he fit in, the way he pitched in, the way he learned. Not just the work but the customs. Why he speaks a mix of Spanish, Portuguese, and English better than most of the family. He sings in a local Welsh choir. None of us know what they're singing about but it's beautiful, well sometimes a little melancholy or war-like."

"Oh, all the men sing, even going to work or coming out of the mine. I think it kept them Welsh and kept the language alive." remarked Mary Pugh. "Now about the wedding, what can I do? There has got to be something I can do or add."

Tying the horse to the ring post, the men climbed down from the surrey. They could see their brides' buggy down the street. The two fathers waiting stolidly for the ladies and mothers too, to come out of the house and get into the surrey.

"It looks like we're right on time," murmured Jamie to Owen, who was checking his suit, dusting off his new shoes on his pant legs. No high-heeled boots today. They looked at each other.

"You ready, Jamie? Let's get in there before the ladies get here."

The best men would have been the two grooms, but as it was a double wedding, they had chosen their brothers for the position. Denis, Jamie's older, married brother, was up by the alter, while David, Owen's brother, was talking to Bronwyn and another of the bridesmaids who had recently caught his attention, as the attendees settled into their seats.

"We'd better get up front," Jamie said, "don't want to give a hint of reluctance."

Owen replied, "No, no, I've been hoping for this since I first met Terrie. There is no hesitation on my part."

The children's choir, (among giggles and craning of necks to see the aisle,) grew silent.

The organ began the prelude as the mothers were seated. Led by the maids of honor, the bridesmaids (which now included Bronwyn), began the slow march down the aisle. The brides appeared, Terrie in white and a lace veil brought from Portugal by her grandmother. Soledad was in an ivory gown which set off her hair, covered by a mantilla that had been worn by two earlier generations. The two fathers, looking solemn but happy, presented their daughters.

The men spoke almost together. They had agreed beforehand to do this. "I, Esteban Silva do give my daughter, Teresa Marie Silva Rose,…"

"I Brian Brandon and my wife Esmeralda, do give Soledad Constance Brandon to …"

From that point on, both grooms admitted to each other that they were in a haze. They responded to words and statements by rote. It wasn't until the rings were exchanged and they were declared husband and wife by both the priest and minister and the "You may kiss the bride," that they came out of their stupor.

They exited to the children's choir singing and the happy sounds of family and friends cheering and   calling out advice and happy thoughts.

They escorted the new brides to the two surreys, polished and decorated with ribbons, bells, and a few tin cans added by the local boys.

The two sets of newlyweds circled the town square as a gesture to the many people outside the church and gathered on front porches and yards. Finally arriving at the large building used jointly by the city and several civic groups and social clubs, the couples descended and entered the hall.

Bombarded by blown-out, colored eggs filled with perfumed confetti, they worked their way to a raised platform, through backslaps, thrust hands, and called out well wishes.

"I didn't realize how many people knew us or liked us," whispered Owen to Terrie.

"Owen, remember, our family has been in California and this area a long time. Between shipping and fishing, my Papa, aunts, uncles, and cousins have dealt with a lot of folks," she replied.

Smiling at everyone, Terrie and Solé stepped onto the platform decorated like a wedding cake and pulled Jamie and Owen up beside them.

Terrie called out over the noisy crowd still entering the building, "Thank you all for your help and attention."

Solé added, "It's beautiful. You make me feel like a Princess in the Arabian Nights, and here is my Prince," getting Jamie to smile and wave at the crowd.

The hall was decorated with garlands and banners, ribbons floating down from the rafters, As they stepped down, a group of musicians came on and began serenading the newly-weds and then switched to reels, schottisches and popular songs. The crowds moved to the seating areas and food, clearing a dance area for those so inclined. As the music tapered out, shouting began for the wedding party to move onto the dance floor.

Owen, looking at a radiant Terrie, said "See if I was a good learner. Let's show them what you taught me," and they stepped out as Jamie and Solé joined them. After a couple of rounds with family joining in, they moved out into the crowd, to greet well-wishers and friends.

The hall had a mix of different foods, reflecting the backgrounds of the participants. Beer and wine was flowing from kegs and casks, with parents monitoring who drank what, frequently directing some to the bowls of fruit punch.

Different music began to come, not only from the raised platform, but also from outside, where others had gathered and even set up some tables to take   advantage of the crowds. Outside a corral had been set up with ponies and burros for the children to ride. Reigning over the scene were General Sherman and Ramona, with ribbons braided into their manes and tails and flower garlands draped over their necks. They were considered by those in the know, as intimate parts in the courtship. Local children clambered over and around them, showing off for their friends.

After the two cakes were cut and handed out, singers took their places on the platforms. The Welsh Chorus began with folk songs and ballads. David, now one of the group, called for Owen to join them. "I know most of you don't

267

know Owen can sing, but he has been part of this group since long before I arrived in California. My brother, Owen Llewellyn Pugh, and a Welsh wedding song."

Blushing slightly, Owen moved onto the stage, "To my darling wife, will she always remember this day." Accompanied by fiddles, flutes, and the chorus, he began in Welsh and after two verses switched to English, then Portuguese.

David whispered to Terrie, "He had this translated for you. My mother and sister helped."

The crowd quieted when Owen's clear tenor voice penetrated the hall, with the soft background accompanying it. As it shifted to English, then Portuguese, the crowd grew more attentive. When it ended, they broke into applause and shrill trills.

Terrie, eyes glistening, spoke quietly to Owen, "That was beautiful, the best wedding present a woman could receive. Thank you, Owen."

As the crowd resumed talking, another group took the stage They were dressed in bright flowery shirts and carried guitars and what looked like mini guitars. Someone called out, "Hey, they've got ukuleles, be quiet."

"Hello. We're from Hawaii. My mates and I have been working on the Silva ranch and boats for a long time, and we would like to celebrate the event and the family's friendliness to us by singing an authentic Hawaiian wedding song and finishing with a ballad." He tapped out a rhythm on a hand drum and the instruments. The soft tones of the Hawaiian language oozed through the hall.

The wedding couples used this lull in activities to escape. "What are you going to do?" asked Owen of Jamie and Soledad.

"Jamie and I have a boat by the pier. We're going there and putting out into the bay."

Jamie said, "We didn't want to be shivareed and disturbed by a rowdy and drunken crowd of friends. What are your plans?"

"I don't know. Terrie set it up and told me nothing. It's to be a surprise." Jamie and Solé got into the buggy and trotted off into the evening.

Terrie came up. "Owen, we're going back to the house. Change into your riding clothes and get Sherman and Ramona. Bring them around back."

Having done as ordered, Owen waited as Terrie appeared wearing her old riding outfit. Climbing onto Ramona, she called out, "Follow me," and took off. Sherman, eager to catch up, whinnied and huffed. Owen climbed on and they took off at a gallop. They followed what was now their regular trail to the spring and forest.

Slowing as they reached the redwoods, Terrie said, "Please stake the horses here and follow me." Owen, following the light of a small lantern, was quickly behind Terrie. As they moved into the familiar area, he saw the gigantic burned out tree before them.

Terrie moved in and stepped aside. "What do you think of our wedding night suite, Owen?"

Lanterns were waiting to be lit. He could see from the small lantern, a bed of boughs and a small feather bed had been set up. Canvas covered the two openings to keep out cold and critters.

"It's perfect, Mrs. Teresa Pugh," Owen replied in a hushed voice.

After a couple of days and nights of love and riding the trails and discussing the future, the newly wed couple cleaned up the camp. Terrie had arranged for some of the hands to remove the remnants of their stay later. She wanted it to be as pristine as possible. Owen brought the horses up for the trip back.

"Owen, help me up. I'm a little sore. You certainly gave me a hard workout for these two days."

"Well Terrie, every time I tried to rest, you rolled onto me. Lady, you wore me out, time after time. I'm so exhausted you may have to saddle the horses yourself." They grinned at each other as Terrie walked to the small fire, where a Dutch oven, and a coffee pot were set to the edge of a steel sheet,

"I don't suppose you have the strength to eat?" Terrie asked. Using an apron draped on a bush, she lifted the lid of the iron pot and pulled two biscuits out. "Freshly baked, you notice, while you dreamed of what you did to me last night, I, like a dutiful wife, got up and made breakfast." She walked to Ramona and Sherman and gave them each a warm biscuit.

"Hey," said Owen, "Don't I deserve one of those?"

"Well, what have you done for me lately? These two have been attentive and nuzzling me all morning."

"If I kiss you and nuzzle you, will I get a biscuit?" replied Owen, grabbing her as she flounced by with a couple of apples for Sherman and Ramona, hugging and kissing her, then carrying her back toward the hollow tree.

"No, you don't, not now anyway. We have to meet Jamie and Solé at the dock. Remember, they have a cruise planned," said Terrie, edging away. "Eat your biscuits, bacon, and eggs before the jays get them."

Nearing the corral and house, they could see a small crowd gathered, friends and family.

"Well, where did you two go? We were all set to give you a noisy send off and you were gone. I think Mama knew where, but she wouldn't tell us. I can't say you look rested. Not much sleep?" asked Mr. Silva, while Mama just blushed.

"Well, if he's like the other Pugh men, I know why he's tired," said David, as his mother shushed him and hit him on the shoulders.

The new brides and the ladies moved into the parlor to discuss things while the men remained in the kitchen. Little was said about the wedding nights as the new husbands were leery about discussing intimate events with their wives' fathers and brothers.

"I won't ask where you're going," Arthur said. "David, the hands, and I can handle the business while you two are gone. Mateo will come over from the fishing boats to handle bay transport. Everything is taken care of.

"Owen, the surprise for Teresa is in the works. It should be ready and going when you get back."

"Thanks, it sounds like everything is under control," replied Owen and Jamie simultaneously.

After lunch the couples climbed into the buggy, followed by a small buckboard loaded with luggage. "Tell the children to be careful with Sherman and Ramona," called back Teresa as they trotted off.

Sitting at the dock was the same boat used when Owen, Jamie, and Teresa, (now permanently "Terrie" to the family), first crossed the bay together.

Newly repainted a shiny white, with polished brass, it had a new name, "Moonstruck," painted on the stern. After loading on the luggage, Jamie maneuvered out to open water, using the engine. Shutting down, Owen appeared from the hold in his knit cap and sailor's gear.

Solé came out of the cabin in a house dress pinned up. Terrie appeared almost as she was when Owen first saw her on the boat, baggy trousers instead of a skirt, rope sandals, and hair falling out from under a knit cap.

"You ladies, help let loose the sail," called Jamie. A glistening white, new sail went rolling up. "Whoa, I didn't expect that," Jamie yelled. On the sail two sets of interlocking red hearts were painted, with a golden 'Jamie and Solé' embroidered on one and 'Owen and Terrie' in the other. A note stitched to the sail read, "From your mothers and sisters, love."

The fog had burned off when they pulled into the harbor. Jamie engaged one of the carters to take them to a small hotel off Union Square, where they settled in.

The first evening, after dinner at Eduardo's, they went to a vaudeville show. An Irish tenor and his troop singled them out and sang a romantic song.

As they were loading the buggy and wagon, the latter with some additional boxes, Terrie sidled next to Owen. Whispering in his ear, she said, "Owen, I'm pregnant."

Hugging her, he replied, "How do you know that? We haven't been married that long."

She said, "I just know. You'll see. A boy or a girl, Owen! Maybe one of each. I'm sure."

When they got back to the now budding new town, or at least settlement, Owen said, "Close your eyes for a minute, and don't open them until I tell you to. I—I guess we, the family, have a surprise for you." The buggy pulled up and stopped. "You can look now."

In the vacant lot, a new storefront was standing. Large glass windows, small tables and a counter were visible. Over the doorway was a large, carved, two-sided rose, bright scarlet with white edges. An ornate sign below it proclaimed, "The Wild Rose Dairy and

Creamery." On the window in gold letters were the words, "Terrie Rose Pugh and Family, Owners and Proprietors."

"What do you think? Are you okay with it? The land your family left is our dairy, and I've been buying and rounding up milk cows for over a month. It opened as soon as we left."

'It's wonderful, Owen, local milkers. I can open an animal park nearby. Take in kittens and puppies. Maybe orphaned goats, sheep, whatever."

Barely nine months later, Arthur Lew (short for Llewellyn) Pugh was born.

Made in USA - Crawfordsville, IN
89389_9798388404008
04.14.2023 1014